Abdallah Uld Mohamadi Bah

Birds of Nabaa
A Mauritanian Tale

Abdallah Uld Mohamadi Bah

Birds of Nabaa
A Mauritanian Tale

Translated from the Arabic by Raphael Cohen

Banipal Books

Birds of Nabaa, A Mauritanian Tale
First published in English translation
by Banipal Books, London, 2023

Arabic copyright © Abdallah Uld Mohamadi Bah
English translation copyright © Raphael Cohen, 2023
Tuyour al-Naba'a was first published in Arabic in 2017
Original title: طيور النبع
Published by Jadawel, Beirut, Lebanon

The moral right of Abdallah Uld Mohamadi Bah to be identified
as the author of this work and of Raphael Cohen as the translator
of this work has been asserted in accordance with the Copyright,
Designs and Patents Act, 1988.

A CIP record for this book is available in the British Library
ISBN 978-1-913043-43-8
E-book: ISBN: 978-1-913043-44-5

Front cover photography courtesy Azouz Begag

Banipal Books
1 Gough Square, LONDON EC4A 3DE, UK
www.banipal.co.uk/banipalbooks/

Banipal Books is an imprint of Banipal Publishing
Typeset in Cardo

Printed and bound in Great Britain by Clays Ltd, Elcograf S.p.A.

CONTENTS

Birds Soaring in Our Sky 1

In the Shade of Teresa 19

Soaring above the Touched Man's Nest 37

My Life as Travelogue 49

Rajab's Shade-Giving Tent 69

Three Men and a Woman 75

Mariam, the Cowrie Shell Reader 77

Abdurrahman Lays down the Saddle 95

War Dance at Kanz al-Asrar 129

That Woman's Name Is Mounira 141

Bread and Mint 153

The Sheikh's Vision Comes True 163

Glossary 175

Biographies of the author and translator 178

Other titles by Banipal Books 180

Birds Soaring in Our Sky

It is well past midnight and I am very nearly asleep, though I am determined to stay awake until the dawn prayer. The noise coming through the window overlooking Madrid's Gran Vía is making my task easier. There is a nightclub directly below the balcony, and I can hear the stamp of dancing feet and Brazilian samba music booming out, interspersed with fleeting gasps and whoops of delight. Something within reminds me of our quiet village and its innocent pleasures, and I long to join the late-night revellers in the dance.

I long for a past among low houses stretching between two hills of soft sand, and for the joy of celebratory days when, to the beat of the tabla, men and women would come together in the dance arena. The women wear deep blue Indian cloth, which casts a tinge on flushed faces and any visible part of amber arms and legs. The men spar in stick dances, each pair seeming to fight, one striving to defeat and kill the other, but the stick staves off any possible harm. At the climax of the dance, trills of joy rise and soar like birds on the wing, echoing be-

1

tween the secluded sand dunes and through Nabaa's
nearer quarters.

Those trills turned Nabaa's festal nights into celebra-
tions, while at the Moulid the spiritual charisma of my
sheikh would pierce the depths of my being and mysterious feelings burst into flame. Then my troubled soul
would open up to the mysteries of its Creator and bodies
would melt in a singular spiritual ecstasy. That was my
first schooling in the carefree life of the vagabond, as
Abdurrahman was wont to describe it.

I liked being a vagabond and it became an ingrained
habit. But only a few local men shared my inclinations,
those whom the learned men of gravitas described as
wrong-headed: rowdy, flighty youngsters who lived
outside familiar conventions and paid little heed to
strong tribal traditions.

Today, far away in Madrid as I prepare to return to
that beautiful world, which sometimes dominates my
thoughts for days, even weeks, I bring my friends to
mind one by one.

How wonderful it is to feel like those wayward ones,
who celebrate life and the pleasures it affords, and to join
them in the same free expression of what is in the mind
and call things clearly by their names without equivo-
cation, hypocrisy, embarrassment or pretence.

Whenever I am stirred by longing and nostalgia, the
image of Nabaa appears. Am I dreaming? I cannot tell.
A mix of faces appears out of the haze. I cannot quite
make out their features, but they are familiar, friendly.

The image of Rajab the teacher emerges. He is putting on his blue *litham*, his face veil, as if a cloud has appeared from nowhere to provide him shade. A leather bag dangling from his shoulder contains the necessaries to make green tea, plus a few of his favourite tapes. He is heading for one of the houses to spend time alone. The glasses of tea, whose strong taste blends with the music of his favourite singer, Mahjouba, are possibly the only things disturbing the clarity of that seclusion.

His image fades and that of Hussein the poet shines in my mind. He is reciting a love poem praising the full figure of a remarkable woman. He describes her as dark velvet, so black that the morning light does not reveal her. Broad and fat, the sight of her brings pleasure. Because of her mountainous flesh she is only able to stand with great difficulty. Neither tall nor short, it is as if she has been carved from beautiful, primordial matter. In his tremulous high-pitched voice, Hussein repeats a line from a famous poem by Kaab ibn Zuhair:

Waif-like advancing, full-figured receding
　　no complaints that she is too tall or too short.

Other faces also appear as if from nowhere. In the flow of images comes my sheikh, the man touched – or as we say, attracted – by the divine energy. He is spinning his whole body, merging with the light breeze to whip up the sand of the dunes behind him. As he dances, he re-cites a poem, twirling his hands to the rhythm as though he wished to catch hold of the music within the letters and words. At the same time, the stamp of his feet on the sand causes it to eddy upwards in cones. The sand whips up more and more and gradually obscures his face.

The images swarm and another man appears. I cannot discern his features clearly enough to reveal his identity: taller than those around him, he is wearing a white turban and a red wrap around his head and face. He is surrounded by a large entourage, also without features, who are dancing and singing on an island surrounded on all sides by water. But the water recedes, leaving only a barren universe without a single drop of water.

I wake from the dream feeling very thirsty. The music rising from the dance club pulsing with life at the heart of Madrid is deafening, and urges me to go in and quench my thirst. Why shouldn't I take the chance to enjoy the happy atmosphere before I leave the city for good?

Sobriety holds me back. Now that I have turned forty, it is no longer seemly to indulge my passions. True, the Madrid night is rowdy and alluring, making it easy to be caught in its seductive web, but since not too long ago I have become used to curbing the unruly passions of my soul and following my rational mind as it urges me to seek calm and tranquillity. Unless of course the Sufi spark dormant in my heart, an ever thirsty and seeking heart, should awaken and ignite the fire.

* * *

4

I have spent ten years in the Spanish capital. The pleasures of life came to me effortlessly. Money flowed through my fingers like a river spilling down a mountain. I spend the pesetas without a second thought. Tonight I complete the eleventh month of my tenth year, and now I speak Spanish, which I learned in the cafés and from listening to the chattering of my Brazilian neighbour, who speaks fluent Castilian.

Tomorrow at dawn, I will take an Iberia Airlines plane to Paris, then a UTA flight to Nouakchott, where the roaring ocean waves crash into the burning desert sands.

Will I be able to bear leaving this enchanting city and begin a new life in what is, compared to clamorous Madrid, not a city?

A week before my departure, I received a letter from a childhood friend, Mohammed Mukhtar. As young companions, together we had often chased through meadows after gazelles. That was before his father brought a Qur'an teacher of Malian origin to live among us. The man's family settled in Nabaa and became part of the tribe.

The embassy postman hands me a buff envelope. I scrutinise the handwritten address before reading the sender's name on the back. The letters and words look as if they are trying to disguise their writer's identity. But it is obviously my friend's handwriting, which has not changed since we studied *hizbs* of the Holy Qur'an, pre-Islamic poems and some elements of grammar together under the touched sheikh.

5

I notice that the postage stamp bears the picture of the parliament building that has just been finished. It is a gift to Mauritania from the People's Republic of China and President Mao.

I am also sure that he has copied the address, which someone wrote in French for him. I left him a decade ago, and all he knew of the language of Molière was his times tables, and the Arabic numerals, which are falsely ascribed to the Romans.

Trembling with fear at the prospect of reading sad news, I open the envelope. I have not received a letter from Mohammed Mukhtar for a few months and have no idea what surprises my friend's letter might contain.

The opening lines prove reassuring. They talked about male and female friends: who had got married and who engaged, which women had given birth and which divorced, which of our companions had recklessly embarked upon a heedless life doing as he pleased. He concluded with news of the marriage of our friend Mohammed Amin, commenting with a flood of emotion that it was "a notable event in Nabaa".

He related how Mohammed Amin had brought a well-known singer to perform at the wedding party. He had, however, had to hide him away in a tent erected a few miles outside the village because the sheikhs, who control every aspect of life in Nabaa, "call this kind of party haram out of fear that men and women will mix, and deem them to be profligate and obscene", as he put it. As expected, our friend tricked the local elite and organised a splendid party with music. The bride's girl-friends sneaked in, and the people of Nabaa enjoyed a night of music and entertainment the likes of which had never been seen before. They even took to using that night to date other events, saying they occurred so many years after Mohammed Amin's wedding.

Following the news of that splendid party into which "joy was smuggled", as he put it, he wrote briefly about his work as a trader in Nouakchott, and then at length about the newly-formed capital, whose foundation stone had been laid by General de Gaulle some twenty years ago.

I yearned for the tiniest details, I who have been hugged so close by Madrid and immersed in its delights; delights I have savoured without limit, in a despairing and futile attempt to fill the emptiness in my soul.

I read and reread Mohammed Mukhtar's letter closely, especially the paragraphs where he sketched the features of the capital, Nouakchott. Deep inside, I hoped to find in it a replacement for the pleasures of life in Madrid that I was going to miss. However, one sentence that Mohammed Mukhtar wrote extra large at the end of the letter struck like a thunderbolt: "There's nothing here except for people's kindness, glasses of green tea and a little music . . ." It was as if through its force, that sentence turned into a blast of burning wind twisting between the large letters. A blast that scorched the depths of my soul and whose intensity pained my heart with longing and nostalgia.

There would be no Madrid life in Nouakchott then. No late nights until the break of a dawn damp with gentle drizzle. No flamenco music that made the kohl-rimmed eyes of Andalusian girls fill with ecstatic tears. No fun and no samba dancing with the Indian-looking Teresa. How then could I adjust to the life of that desert capital city, so unlike other capital cities, and whose residents were not used to going out to restaurants, or even drinking coffee in the morning?

I arrived at Nouakchott Airport shortly before sunset. Having flown through a sandstorm, the UTA DC10 landed on a runway just finished by a French construction company, and which the sandstorm had nearly turned into a graveyard.

The city, where rainfall was rare, greeted me from under a film of darkish dust, and it was hard to distinguish my family among the welcoming crowds, but relatives hugged me with a delight exuding from dusty, veiled faces. Layers of dust formed miniature sand dunes amid folds of cloth above eyes moist with longing, and it seemed that the sorely needed rain was reflected in those glistening, welcoming eyes.

They had come from Nabaa. None of them wanted to miss this opportunity. I knew the hardships of the journey to the city for a clan of brothers and cousins, but they had taken the decision to come. I had no choice but to submit to their wishes; wishes that revealed their true character, which neither dust nor sand could conceal.

Photographs of me wearing elegant suits had already

reached them. Although it was not my habit, I had taken pictures of myself in various poses in the streets, parks and restaurants of Madrid. In doing so, I wanted to give them a clear and candid impression of my old life there, in an earthly paradise where water, greenery and the fine façades of opulent Gothic buildings all mixed together. With those photographs, perhaps I gave an opening to their innocent curiosity that fed a desire to discover more. For them, my world went beyond their wildest imaginings.

Despite the absence of Andalusian architectural features and the delight they brought to the soul, or perhaps because of it, all the people of Nabaa, so I was told, invited each other to look at the photographs, which circulated among them. They showed glamorous worlds that fired a sense of baffled amazement. The photographs, and the sight of this man from the desert wearing European dress just like a European, even with necktie, filled their hearts with astonishment. The pictures provided them with a documentary summary of my new life in an alien land, and no doubt served as first-hand evidence that I, in contrast to so many others, was still alive and well. For decades the people of Nabaa had endured the slow haemorrhage of migration and been lost in a maze of unanswerable questions. What had become of all those who had not died, their fates unknown? Many had never sent word nor left any trace, not a single sign of their being in some foreign land. Their images were no longer under control, just like the changes to their way of life. Alive or on the verge of death, it made no difference. But in their view, by virtue of these photographs, I was the exception that proved the rule.

The pictures were conclusive proof of my existence: in colour, and full of joy and life, like photos of a child on his birthday preening in his new outfit, unable to conceal his pride in himself. Perhaps they were also photographs that gave a clear and defined impression of the fake glamour of the world I was living in, or trying to, without completely shedding the desert sand settled inside me, which has become part of who I am.

The welcoming committee embraced me as I made my way out of the diminutive airport, which comprised only two small halls. Mohammed Mukhtar was there with his white Peugeot 504 that I had shipped to him a year before from the Spanish port of Algeciras across the sea from Morocco. The car's Spanish number plate was just as I had left it, and getting that through Customs had been an additional expense. Mohammed Mukhtar was also still counting on my generosity to finish the procedures. I haven't forgotten till now that during a rare telephone conversation he said to me: "There'll be the chance to sell it and make a profit . . ."

I thought it was about time I took a break from his money-making schemes. No question, I was his goose that lays the golden eggs. And he got the eggs whenever and however he wanted: today the car, yesterday the shop. There was nothing to suggest that the golden opportunities he was always writing to me about were ever serious. Even my family suspected that what I sent via him only reached them sporadically.

Mohammed Mukhtar was the link between two worlds. He was the first of us to become a businessman in the capital and learn the ins-and-outs of commerce. He was the first to have a mailbox and a telephone. In a dark corner of that shop he owned in the capital, in the booth constructed specially for the purpose, everyone would receive their calls.

I knew my ability to make money did not equate to half his ability to spend it. I constantly frittered money away without thinking about it, and took great pleasure in doing so. It had been an ingrained behaviour since I was small, and I was unable to drop the habit when I grew up, learned the importance of economy and became an accountant. Perhaps I inherited that part of my character from my grandmother, who had warned me against the seduction of money and instilled in me a fear of the fate of the rich. She told me the story of Qarun whom, by divine command, the ground swallowed up along with his house. I often heard her say in her prayers: "O Lord, O Lord, by the Sura of the Sand Dunes, be generous and give us barely enough."

God had undoubtedly answered her prayers, for I tried hard to save some of my monthly salary and what was left over from the ambassador's expenses, but those savings soon evaporated, sometimes because of my own casual fancies, but more often because of Mohammed

Mukhtar's delusional schemes, which he tricked me into.

I have to forget about him and stop his phantasmagorical schemes. I have to wipe from my memory the Peugeot parked on the side of the road gathering dust and rusting away. I have to turn a page on every thought that spoils my mood and stops me enjoying my short leave, my first break in ten years I am spending among family and friends.

True, the Spanish pesetas are all I have left of the bundles of foreign currency that I brought with me. I've kept five hundred thousand and sent them to the Central Bank to be exchanged. It's also true that the black market is still unheard of in our youthful capital, but I'm not sorry about that. The amount of CFA Francs that my brother Ahmed came back with will be more than enough.

On the evening of my arrival in Nouakchott, I was lucky enough to witness a glitzy party marking the launch of our national currency, held at the Ahmedi Hotel, the city's grandest hotel at the time. Back then, the presence of a hotel built in partnership with a Moroccan businessman on the shores of the Atlantic, where cool breezes mix with at times the burning breath of the desert, represented the continuing urban development of the capital and its openness to the deep blue sea. And because the capital had suddenly set her face towards the sea, bracing her chest to its stormy blue, eyes had got used to that building which, gradually and cautiously, pierced our calm sky. It was as if our eyes –

accustomed to the vast open expanses of the Sahara –
were betraying us in various ways for unknown reasons.
The hotel was also a hub for politicians and businessmen,
and a base for visiting foreign delegations.

Mohammed Mukhtar, along with other friends, suggested that we sneak into the concert being given by the
singer Sidati. It wasn't hard to get past security, which
consisted of three exhausted policemen, all dazzled by
the opulence on display. So we sneaked into the main
hall, where we saw senior officials, ministers and bureau-
crats, together with their wives, in a self-congratulatory
moment which somehow seemed timeless.

The singer Sidati, holding a four-stringed *tidinet*, stood
on the small wooden stage. That night he sang like
never before while strumming the rectangular instrument.

Ministers wearing black and navy blue dinner jackets
and bow ties danced in circles that opened up and closed
in. Accompanying them to the rhythm, which was familiar to me, was the President's French wife Marie-
Thérèse. In her hand she was holding a full glass of a
brown liquid, as were a number of the ministers. The
President stood watching the astonishing scene as he enjoyed a glass of green tea with wild mint.

To me the party seemed to reveal what had changed
about Nouakchott's culture and its new government.
The men in their black or navy suits were like birds flitting about in a sparkling Parisian sky, yet the gloss of
their polished black shoes would vanish as soon as they

stepped out into the sand-laden streets.

Government ministers wore civilised dress – what they call "Christian" clothes – while the mass of the people shunned such clothing, being content with their traditional robes, whose riot of colour was brighter than that of the newly-built market in the heart of the capital. A veritable sea of colours: white, blue and black dotted with others from the heart of the African continent and its tropical zones, like a painting by Matisse, its still-life details infused with the heat of life itself.

Mohammed Mukhtar then took me on a tour to rediscover this new city, which had developed not far from the Atlantic coast, calling to mind the prophecy of a holy man who had said the city would become very populous and then suffer destruction. It was just that nobody knew when fate would execute this harsh sentence.

The tour began with a visit to Mohammed Mukhtar's shop in the new market. No doubt he wanted to persuade me that the money I had assiduously sent him had not gone to waste, and he began to give me lessons in investment, as though he were the reincarnation of Adam Smith founding the theory of capital and surplus value. This first performance cost us nothing, and Mohammed Mukhtar remained happy since I did not go into his accounts too closely.

We continued the tour of the city's landmarks. The transformations, which I was seeing for the first time, were astonishing. I felt like a child exploring with racing heart an imagined city, stumbling between dreams and dust.

An open space was full of young men arguing at the tops of their voices. Curiosity compelled me to draw near one of the circles. It was a group of students with passionate views, loudly debating with each other in small groups. I sensed that my friend was going to force me into an argument that I had no wish to get involved in, so I tried to retreat. Then a young man pulled at my arm. He was wearing a *dura'a* and carrying a pile of Egyptian newspapers with pictures of Gamal Abdel Nasser on the front pages. He started talking to me about the One Arab Nation that stretched from the Ocean to the Gulf. A nation whose unity had been sundered by colonialism and imperialism! He spoke quickly and excitedly as if he wanted to give me a crash course in the foundations of Arab nationalism. Once I had disentangled my arm from him, another young man, who had been observing the scene, said to me politely: "Don't listen to him. Watch out, he's spreading chauvinist ideas and threatening national unity."

The dispute between the two young men escalated into a violent argument. Others joined in, voices were raised, and blows were nearly exchanged.

"We have to leave," said Mohammed Mukhtar. "Soon this lot will start fighting, their loyalties divided among Gamal Abdel Nasser, Michel Aflaq, Mao Zedong and the legacy of Senghor." The last was a reference to the young Africans who adopted black nationalist ideas.

We were in the vacant lot adjoining the Ministry of

Education, which in its rowdiness and the variety of subjects up for trenchant debate, resembled the Speakers' Corner of London's Hyde Park. The circles of young men asked us to stay and join in. They were all students, waiting in front of the Ministry for the decision on sending them to university abroad. They spent all day in endless political debates, in which each faction hoped to attract more supporters to its ideas. There were Baathists, Nasserites and "Toilers", a reference to the Communist Party or the "lumpen proletariat" as their opponents called them. As for me, I found following this silly irrational sophistry deadly boring.

I wanted to discover the hidden, veiled face of Nouakchott. Another face that the sand had covered and obscured, cloaking it in stubborn mystery. A shy face, especially at night, about which much had been said to me. I thirsted to get to know it up close and plunge into its depths.

My friend promised me a tour of the musicians' houses. That was the only space open to the stream of talent in poetry, music and song that flowed into the capital every day from the countryside and the desert. It drew inspiration from the pain and sorrow of new immigrants and gave the growing city a new spirit.

Nouakchott consisted of two large districts: the old city, whose major features the French had planned but never finished building, and the new city, which the Mauritanians had built but not planned. Between the two cities/districts lay a stretch of flat, sandy ground.

Hundreds of Bedouin, whose herds had been decimated by drought and who had been forced to migrate to the city, had made a beeline for it. Among these new arrivals came families from the class of singers who had inherited the profession down the generations.

Tents and houses were opened for sessions during Nouakchott's refreshing nights, while receptive hearts, stirred from time to time by the Atlantic breeze, opened up to imbibe those rare pleasures.

A female singer sat cross-legged on a vast rug surrounded by young men. She held an *ardeen*, a harp-like instrument played by women, with long strings and brass rings that would reverberate as the rhythm was set. The first string started to vibrate, perhaps trembling in delight at the touch of slender fingers, as she delicately played a tune that Zaryab – who, it was said, had forgotten his oud in Chinguetti – might have left behind.

The singer sang a line of heroic martial poetry. Her beautiful voice split the calm and silence of the night. Layers of melody flowed until almost dawn, crossing the silent regions of the night, whose star-studded heavens looked down, invoking all the heroic and romantic poetry produced by the Arab tribes in their age of glory.

Competitions started up between the young poets to see who could come up with the finest impromptu poetry. The session continued until the dawn call to prayer, before the night sky lightened, when the revellers tripped lightly off, having downed dozens of glasses of the green tea offered in the venues for free as an act of hospitality.

There were several female singers. Manina, who sang in her sad voice of Laila's Majnoun. Mahjouba, who sang "Areet" (a corruption of the French word arreter), a new number about the French Peugeot cars that carried passengers around the new capital and which Nouakchott had not known before. Niama, who bewailed the fortune of the Barmakids in Baghdad, and perhaps my fortune too in Madrid's Gran Vía.

Nouakchott's innocent night carried me along, in the company of my group of friends. We competed with others to recite lines of poetry in that unique atmosphere, indifferent to the surprises an iniquitous fate held in store.

In the Shade of Teresa

My Saharan days go by, slow and dull. There is nothing to revitalise my spirits apart from reading poetry, which shatters stagnant time, and drifting along in my memories. It looks like I still miss the Madrid I left: the morning coffee with bread and butter and the sight of the trim Colombian waitress as she outdid the others to serve me my fresh orange juice with one ice cube and a smile as wide and bright as the sky.

I had worked as an accountant in Madrid, but I had never had absolute authority over the figures. I would just check the expenses and make sure they conformed to regulations, sort and bundle up the invoices, and forward them to the Ministry via the diplomatic bag.

Work at the Embassy was routine, and if I am honest my only task was to tally up His Excellency the Ambassador's interminable and inexhaustible expenses. The man knew that the Foreign Ministry was generous with him, so whenever he needed more, he added another line item to the budget, which the comptroller-general at the Foreign Ministry would sign off. The money, of course, came regularly and on time, never late. At the end of every month, however, we would find that half the allocated budget had not been spent. Then we would meet up to devise ways to spend what remained. His Excellency the Ambassador would take the lion's share; I would watch him pick up the bundles of notes without so much as batting an eyelid. I did regret this turn of events, and something in me did die, although I benefitted enough from it to help me counteract the tedium of my Madrid apartment.

On Sundays I would invite round those neighbours and fellow Mauritanians with whom I was friendly. We amused ourselves playing cards and in witty repartee until the afternoon, when a roast Andalucian lamb would be set on the table, straight out of the local baker's oven, pristine and untouched. The delicious aroma of roast meat filled our nostrils and we lost interest in playing cards. My neighbour, Teresa, whom I had taught the art of roasting and mixing the spices in our Saharan way, would burst into a gypsy song about blood, betrayal, abandonment and other things unknown to me, as she hovered around us like a butterfly drawn to a flame. From time to time we stared at her with eyes of wonder, desirous of the fire smouldering in her songs, while, moving as lightly between us as a fresh breeze, she laid her delicious dishes on the table.

At first, Teresa found these gatherings an unpardonable extravagance. Once when I was getting ready to host my friends on a Friday evening, she approached me in a state of semi-undress, wearing only a thin white shirt, which covered her breasts but barely reached her smooth, rosy navel, and shorts that revealed the fullness of her thighs. When she moved, the shorts slipped down a little but never as far as her ivory knees. Teresa tossed her head like a nervous filly due to go out to breed, and her long, perfumed hair filled the room with the scent of orange blossom. I was wowed by her, and almost yielded to her seduction in that rundown apartment at the heart of amorous Madrid.

One morning Teresa heard me talking to the Spanish butcher of Moroccan origin. I was asking him to get us a fat lamb and roast it in the oven. She interrupted me, and said firmly: "What, for God's sake, are you going to do with all that meat? You must be some species of carnivorous rodent."

"Yes, indeed, my good lady," I responded. "And we compete with the wolves for stray sheep."

She laughed and said: "Try to eat more fruit and vegetables."

"But only animals eat plants," I said, adding: "After your advice, perhaps you might be able to help us get things ready for Sunday's party."

"Yes, I might," she said politely. "To work then."

Teresa burst into my life without prior warning. Coincidence prompted the relationship, which seemed a mixture of affection, concealed infatuation and sibling love. All those feelings combined, just as in some Spanish cities the sun shone, rain showered and snow fell, all on the same day.

* * *

When I first arrived in Madrid, I lived at a small hotel not far from the Embassy. Spain was under the rule of General Franco, and the wounds of the Civil War had yet to heal. Nonetheless, life in Madrid embraced anything new. The city breathed alternately hot and cold from one mouth: it remembered the agonies of the war, whose fires still burned within perplexed hearts. But those fires were soon tempered during the residents' late nights out in search of pleasure and oblivion. It seemed evasion was the path to salvation.

An old married couple ran the hotel. They seemed destined soon to descend from the tiring train of life, but resisted by snatching sporadic moments of pleasure in the time that remained to them. Their young and wild daughter helped them, drifting here and there without purpose.

When I arrived, the old lady, with a pale smile that soon became one of encouragement, handed me the key to a room on the first floor. The room was airy and overlooked a well-lit narrow alley whose ancient-looking walls were adorned with hanging baskets of flowers. On the whole they were very kind to me.

On Sundays, I was their guest for a meal of paella (whose name derives from the Arabic *ba'aya* – leftovers) which it is said was created by our ancestors, the Arabs. Andalucian paella is a mixture of fish, seafood, chicken, rice and vegetables all seasoned with saffron, other spices and olive oil. They set up the dining table in the hallway outside their room, whose doors and windows were wide open to the sunlight. Another small table with a mosaic top would usually be set in the middle for glasses of cold water and fresh juice from the oranges the old lady brought from a farm not far from Madrid.

We ate the delicious food, skilfully made by the old lady in copious quantities. This was the couple's way of spending the profits of their work at the hotel. They were generous with themselves, and with me as well, every Sunday. I was content to share their happiness with a look of gratitude and some words of thanks that made them happy and refreshed the hearts of the kind old couple, along with their daughter.

They placed my seat next to their rebellious, quarrel-some daughter who had a shiny forehead and untidy curly hair. She was usually calmer in the morning, but by the evening, once the sun had set and darkness spread its wings over the corners of the hotel, she would be seized by bouts of hysterical laughter, perhaps because of all the alcohol she drank, secluded in her room, or of being under the influence of the drugs she took in se-cret.

Having completed my first year at the Santa Mañana Hotel, I knew it had become part of me. It lived inside me just as I lived within it, as if I were the warder and it was a prisoner hard to set free. All the same, one autumn day the time came to bid farewell to the owners. I had started to speak rudimentary Spanish, but whatever I was unable to convey verbally, I tried to communicate using sign language.

I spoke to the old couple with the utmost politeness, but my voice was unable to conceal my awkwardness and embarrassment. "This marks the end of happy days. It's time for me to move on . . ."

The day I left the hotel was one to remember. As they said goodbye, I could sense the real affection they had for me. The old lady cried hot tears while her daughter observed stoically from a distance, as if she had shed an existential burden and would now rest easy knowing that the man who could tell tales on her was gone. I departed, leaving her there to her indifference and juvenile fantasies.

The elderly couple accompanied me to the front door. A taxi was waiting for me outside. I had packed my few possessions and personal papers in a leather Samsonite bag, which I had bought from a luxury department store and now placed in the boot of the taxi. As we took off for my new apartment in the centre of Madrid, I turned to wave to the elderly couple and imprint a final image of the farewell in memory. I saw the couple hugging their daughter, who was distraught and in tears. I had never expected that and found it hard to believe. I was amazed by how attached she had become to her Saharan next-door neighbour who paid her very little attention.

But there was nothing I could do, and as I waved good-bye I felt emptiness swell inside me. "Farewell then," I thought. "Sorry for such a big misunderstanding, my little one."

Thanks to a rental agency, I found my new apartment on the Gran Vía. Gran Vía was known as the Broadway of Madrid, after New York's famous artistic and theatre district, but unlike Broadway, Gran Vía had been built in the nineteenth century, but had not taken on its final form until the 1920s. Even its name kept changing in line with the changes in Spanish politics. The most provocative of those names came from the Left during the Civil War, when it was called Soviet Union Street. Then it reverted to its old name after Franco's victory. Gran Vía remains one of Madrid's most important and liveliest thoroughfares. With its high-class shops, nightclubs, restaurants and bars, it is renowned as the only place in Madrid that never sleeps.

What made me anxious during my first night in the apartment was the nightclub right beneath my window. While it might sometimes be blaring out nice music, it was annoying in summer when the pavement in front was turned into an open-air dance floor and, like it or not, I was drawn into the noise.

After being there a couple of months, a single woman moved into the neighbouring apartment. She turned up at the building early one morning just as I was getting ready to go out to work. She wished me a good morning and asked me if I was the "*moro*" who lived in flat number 4. She was unsteady and stumbling with a heavy pack on her back. Her eyes were red with tiredness from a journey that had lasted, she told me later, more than twenty hours. At the rental agency, they had told her that her neighbour was a "good *moro*".

When I came back that evening, she was sound asleep, as demonstrated by her snoring, which I could hear through the partition wall. I wanted to welcome her, as demanded by her rights as a neighbour, rights which my grandmother had versed me in.

The next day, again as I was getting ready to leave for the Embassy, I became better acquainted with my new neighbour. She was sitting at a small café on the corner and I wished her good morning: "*Hola. Buenos días,*" drawing inspiration from my new role as the good *moro*, as propounded by the rental agency.

"I'm Teresa. Why don't you join me?" she responded politely. Then she asked me to have breakfast with her. We sat facing each other across the table, she with her bitter black coffee, me with my coffee-infused milk.

She talked, skipping from topic to topic and occasionally breaking off to chat with the waiter about the weather, poverty, music and the military dictatorship. I loved the way she drank her coffee, taking pleasure as she delayed finishing her cup, sucking up the last drop of the dark liquid as if she were a bee supping nectar. When she bit her full lips, she reminded me of one of our Saharan neighbours, a woman who so loved tea that she would cradle her cup in her hands for ages. That annoyed my grandmother, who was quick to anger and slow to cool.

Teresa gripped the cup as if she were afraid it might slip from her grasp. She drank the dark liquid with relish, as if to say: I'm drinking my coffee, but it's actually you who's enjoying it! She told me her life story in less than thirty minutes, including that she had been a philosophy student and finished her BA some time ago. She had returned from her country of Brazil to settle in Spain after one of her professors had found her a job at a record production company.

I approved of my neighbour's profession, for she spent most of her time listening to the folk music of different ethnic groups, which was what the company specialised in.

"No doubt," I said, "they look to buy the rights from unknown artists at a knockdown price, then sell the records for ten times the price, no?"

She smiled and her eyes glinted craftily as she said in a conspiratorial tone: "Perhaps what you say is right. Who knows . . ."

Teresa told me the last record the company had produced was – what a coincidence – from the country of the *moro*. She wasn't sure whether *moro* here meant Morocco or Mauritania, but I subsequently learnt the identity of the music that had brought Teresa closer to my country and whose melodies had transported her with pleasure.

In the evening, Teresa brought me a CD whose sleeve

bore pictures of women wrapped in black and seemingly playing the tabla. In the centre of their circle was a thin man wearing a blue *dura'a* that billowed upwards. In his raised hand he held a stick that was bent at the end, which served to underline the title in Spanish: "Songs of the Namadi".

We put the CD into the new Sony player and I began listening to songs for dancing, punctuated with ululations and women's voices. Teresa asked me if I knew the group. "It's not a group exactly," I said. "It's the spontaneity of Sahara dwellers, who turn the most ordinary occasion into a big party, with a few gathered together into a pop group."

"Who are these Namadi? Are they one of your main tribes?"

"No, they're made up of different tribes but united by being hunters. They live in the desert expanse of the border region between Morocco, Mauritania and Algeria." I pondered the alert amazement in her eyes and continued: "They live by hunting gazelle with the help of their Sloughi hounds. They think of their dogs as their real wealth and as such even get included in a bride's dowry."

She seemed astonished as she tried to absorb the combination of hunting, music and greyhound breeding. It whetted her appetite to learn more about the inhabitants of the Sahara.

We swayed, enraptured, and our fingers brushed as we listened to the dance music that spoke of love, hunting dogs and dried gazelle flesh. She gave me a look whose meaning I could not fathom, and I returned it with a questioning gaze. And that was enough for both of us!

After that, the records produced by the Madrid company became my companions. I befriended them in my exile, and along with other music, I was attracted to a world that moved my Sufi state of being, only known to those whose souls have yearned for the vast space of the desert and whose spirit has inhabited the space between doubt and certitude. Perhaps Teresa, with her ethereal soul, dwelt in that world with me.

Teresa went on to give me yoga classes. She said yoga helped her forget her poverty and exhaustion. I tried it for a while, before realising that I already possessed spiritual exercises that spared me the need to sit Buddha-like or delve into Taoist teachings.

Over time, Teresa would come to help me run my house. I taught her how to make tea, going deeply into its every ritual, starting with the three glasses of different strength and taste, about which they say the first is as strong as love, the second as sweet as life, and the third as pale as death. I found it impossible to imagine that Teresa might ever drink from that third cup.

I was already in receipt of a monthly ration of green tea, since His Excellency the Ambassador instructed it be sent specially from Nouakchott inside the diplomatic bag. By means of this magical tea, Teresa and I changed places. The tea helped her draw closer to the desert with its scents and rituals, and her obsession with making tea and roasting meat only grew. For my part, I integrated into my new dwelling under her pleasant shade, and life unfolded with her joyous spirit.

From the time in the eighteenth century when Moroccan merchants first brought tea to parts of the Sahara, that beverage had become our companion wherever we went. We could gauge its quality from its scent and would leave it in its pack inside the metal box until it matured. We were addicted to drinking it at breakfast, after lunch, and in the afternoon, like the English gentry. To keep affection flowing, Teresa learned to make tea for us whenever possible. It was as if her heart no longer belonged to her, and as if we had become part of her tribe. Perhaps her Latin blood had transmuted into the tea of the desert, flowing though her veins and leading her down labyrinths until she reached the sands at the heart of the Sahara.

Although I taught Teresa how to choose the best mint from the Moroccan neighbourhood, the real difficulty came in how to sit when preparing tea. Yoga helped with that, together with some photos from a tourism campaign for Mauritania that I picked up in the office of the tourism attaché, charged with promoting a country rarely visited by flights. I asked her to sit with her back straight, as if imitating the cross-legged pose of the Buddha, to relax, go deep inside herself and imagine that she was in eternal nothingness. She had to concentrate on the making of the tea as her one and only task. Then she would attain nirvana, the state of celestial bliss reached only by the pure. Alternatively, she should at least try to imagine herself making paella, a dish requiring a mixture of different ingredients with contrasting tastes and flavours, but whose ultimate aim is a moment of harmony and synthesis between opposites, so that we attain the peaks of both flavour and enjoyment. Finally, I told her that the most important thing about teamaking was to do it with panache. "For *moro* women, teamaking is a form of seduction, one of the rituals of love," I added playfully.

Over time, her training began to bear fruit. Teresa was drawn fully into her new role as domestic help, housewife and extraordinary plenipotentiary friend. She made the tea, roasted the meat and cleaned the house. In return, I helped her make ends meet at the end of the month when money was tight.

On Sundays, Teresa would assume her place in the living room like a Tuareg princess. I had provided her with a dark, almost black, indigo wrap, and she looked stunning wearing the loose garment. Using her skilled hands, she would make the tea, indeed with panache, reworking the foam as I had taught her, to finish with a sponge-like block atop the concentrated infusion.

At times her dominant presence made her seem like a woman from Tiris, that extension of the Sahara from northern Mauritania to the edge of the Draa Valley in Morocco.

Who said that this Brazilian girl, with her lovely light brown skin, was not related to those tribes that dwelt in part along the Atlantic coast? Nomads, they encountered the first Europeans to set foot on Mauritanian soil. Had one of them travelled in the opposite direction and ventured to marry a Portuguese woman? Anything was possible. Indeed, she herself knew only that her parents were of Portuguese descent and that she had been born in Brazil like most of its population.

She liked to believe the account that her roots might reach back to the Sahara, and her involvement with all kinds of African music increased her appetite to read and discover. She devoured travel literature and the accounts of European explorers, especially those from Portugal, who in the fourteenth century had been among the first to penetrate the region and write about it.

Through Teresa I first heard about the ship *La Mendes,* which was driven by the raging Atlantic currents onto the Mauritanian coast laden with exotic cargo. The Saharan tribes welcomed it with great joy and saw its goods as permitted bounty sent by God: sugar, tea, cloth, and best of all, white-skinned slaves fit for all kinds of forced labour.

I expressed my astonishment at what I was hearing, but Teresa looked me straight in the eye as she finished her tale of *La Mendes*. "Spanish and Portuguese for the most part, those white men were turned into prisoners and slaves. That happened when the Europeans ruled the world's seas through conquest and trade and were seeking influence and wealth through every type of force."

She then brought her face so close to mine that I nearly

drowned in the colour of her eyes and the touch of her breath, and added: "Do you know that the kings of Portugal encouraged piracy and spent a great deal of money on shipbuilding and enlisting crews? They would raid the *moro* tribes and take them as pale-skinned slaves whom they sent to their colonies, especially Brazil. That was Portugal's only chance to compete with the other European nations busy colonising and trading. The Portuguese took control, perhaps with the help of those slaves, of parts of Indonesia, Brazil, Macau and many parts of Africa. Unfortunately, however, they took their bad habits with them and taught the colonised peoples to drink, gamble and commit incest. Look at me, my dear, I am part of that cruel history, love it or hate it."

Teresa did not tell me much about her family in Brazil. There was something about her relationship with her parents that she did not want to reveal. Was it because she had been conceived in an illicit union between a Portuguese man and a dark native woman? I don't know, but I do know that she rarely spoke about her father and had a closer relationship with her mother. For my part, I was outside the confusion that enveloped her life.

Reaching out to embrace Teresa, I said to her: "I accept you as you are. Perhaps your blood is mixed with the blood of my ancestors. Perhaps, unbeknown to me, you are my cousin." Our lips met for the first time and we got lost in each other's embrace.

* * *

My relationship with Teresa stretched over a number of years. I loved her truly, and my love would have been entirely platonic except for a few moments of weakness when the devil incited me, but which I regretted. I told her many stories of the great Arab lovers whose passion drove them to madness, or death in the best of cases. I often thought of marrying her, but it wasn't to be. The chains of Bedouin society are unbreakable, even if largely invisible.

I pondered the social consequences awaiting me if I were to bring a Brazilian girl – of dubious origins to boot – home with me to the conservative Saharan milieu and try to implant her in a social environment that gave overriding importance to kinship, genealogy and pedigree. My uncle might rebuke me with hurtful words and refuse to shake my hand. My father might even slap me in the face and kick me out of the house. Only Rajab the teacher would side with me, and that would be out of gleeful spite towards the people of Nabaa. He might even add Teresa to his own band of lovers!

In the period leading up to my departure for Nouakchott, I tried to contain the despondency I felt in the midst of Madrid's rowdy clamour. Then Teresa came to see me and ask for my advice about getting married to a new boyfriend. Holding my arm, she came straight out with it: "While sometimes there seems no prospect of love, I'm always looking, and now, would you believe it, I've found love."

I knew that both of us were looking for love, and had found it together, living there between us in familiarity and friendship. So, as if in response to a question hanging unanswered in the air, I said: "True. Sometimes there is no prospect of love, and that applies to me too."

I gave my blessing to Teresa's union with the young Spanish man who worked at the nightclub under my window. He was tall and muscular, his powerful limbs tattooed with scorpions, snakes and fire-breathing dragons. In contrast, I bore Teresa's name etched in my heart, and neither water nor fire could erase it.

The last time I saw her, Teresa said to me: "Look at him. Fernando is a nice guy and wouldn't hurt a fly. I've tried him and I think he's right for me, but unfortunately he doesn't like tea." She laughed, then leaned towards Fernando and disappeared into his arms as she embraced him so tightly he was unable to free himself. He just looked around, then leaned into her with a look of admiration. That was my last meeting with them, and I closed the chapter on my residence in Madrid.

Soaring above
the Touched Man's Nest

I've been away from kin and country for a long time
– ten years' absence is no easy matter. Is it possible
to hitch a ride through time to reinstate and revive
faces and words that have been lost to the dust? My links
with Nabaa, playground of my youth and home to those
I loved, stretch so far back into the past that I am afraid
they might have been broken and that even memory itself might be fading.

In an effort to order the details of the past, I try to vi-
sualise scenes. The things I remember seem to be broken
into blurry fragments deep in the folds of memory. I try
to coax them out of a dark void and reanimate them, like
a photographer developing a strip of film in a bath of
chemicals, so that images of dazzling whiteness and brilliant colour come through, full of life.

When I left Nabaa behind me to languish in the basket
of oblivion, the place was no more than a few houses
hidden away beneath a layer of dust. Their roofs were
curved to withstand sandstorms and their doors were

open to the winds from the south, from which caravans came laden with grain, tea and sugar. Nabaa seemed to arise each day and brush off the remnants of those sand-laden winds, before vanishing again under the same sand when it sank into silence to await the next storm: an endless cycle that left its existence wavering between presence and vanishing.

Later on, those few houses required a mosque with enough space for more people. A spacious room was built out of cement, limestone and black mud. Next to it rose up something like a small minaret, atop of which ran a balcony overlooking the vast expanse, but to us of course the minaret seemed to touch the clouds in the sky. Then a carpenter came from the nearest town, bringing with him planks of wood, a long saw and a hammer and nails. The ever-veiled imam specified the dimensions of the minbar: no higher than a medium-size chair to match the man's diminutive stature. He also specified the direction for prayer. All of that was a sign that Nabaa had become a true village. One where old men would leave their homes and slowly make their way through dusty alleyways towards the mosque to magnify God, pray and discuss worldly affairs.

Before we settled the question of whether we would live in tents made from black wool or in modern houses made of cement, we had been a lost band. When the community shifted from the nomadic life in search of pasturelands to a sedentary existence, we became strangers to our own language and customs. We said goodbye forever to that temporary village made up of transportable tents, which had not not blown down by sandstorms but whose tent pegs were pulled out in response to the inscrutable instincts of the herds. We packed up our tents and set off behind them in search of pasture and water, heading blindly behind our herds, which were our whole life.

In fact, when the wind carried the scent of grass and of water flowing down scars in the earth to the south, it was the herds that migrated. We just followed them. The only thing that sometimes delayed us was having to fold up the tents and pack up our few belongings. The variation of the tents was ultimately a reflection of the wealth and status of their owners. Tents of different size corresponded to the numbers of family members and their social status. All the tents had distinctive colours, making them seem to assume the features of their owners, whether they were stitched from white canvas or woven from black lambswool.

As part of a community constantly migrating according to the mysterious instincts of the herds, we lived our early childhoods under open skies. We ate, drank, played games and learned the Qur'an, all the while awaiting the next sandstorm. We had no problem with physical space. We owned the horizon, journeying beyond it at the time of our choosing in search of new land for our tents. That land would become our homeland for a period, before we left for another homeland in God's vast world.

Wherever we went, our herds followed, or rather, we followed them. It was their need that determined when and where we had to go.

Whenever we departed, we took with us the books and manuscripts of our founding father. We put them in large, well-locked wooden chests, in which jurisprudence mixed with poetry, genealogy and fortune telling. Also among our things were the wooden boards we smeared with mud before writing on them with a stylus made from a sumac twig, and the essential belongings of the Qur'an teacher.

The journey would last several months, during which we would search for pasture, following the traces of the showers in the rainy season. We would head south to the forests, then track back north as far as the edge of the Greater Sahara, before returning to Nabaa in the summer when the heat was fierce and water from the springs dried up. It was then that we encamped around the well that symbolised the tribe's wealth, its strength and autonomy. The well had been dug by the founding father, in this place on the desert margin where nothing grew apart from thorn trees, tamarisk, and a few lote trees.

The founding father's choice of site was not entirely his own. Rather, history and geography chose it for him, creating the conditions for his forced migration to this remote place, hundreds of miles from his birthplace, where he had once lived safe and sound among family and friends.

Back then, that thick-bearded man of medium height,

who had been a judge in his town, had objected to an absurd conflict that had erupted among his people. The townsfolk spent all day pelting each other with arrows and stones, then when it was time to pray, they formed ranks behind the imam at the mosque as if nothing had happened.

This war continued for ten years, alternately flaring up and dying down. The appeals of the judge did not succeed in halting the war of arrows or in bringing about peace and brotherhood. Once he realised that his appeals were as weak as a voice lost in the wilderness, he decided to leave, setting his face towards the harsh wastes of the southern Sahara in an gesture of remonstrance and anger.

The judge of Chinguetti loaded his books onto camels, a caravan of more than twenty, some said, and arrived more than one thousand miles away at the place that had agreed to give him refuge, on the conditions he himself had determined in advance. His renown preceded him to the tribes of the south, and each one of them hoped to welcome him. He was, after all, coming from a land where knowledge and culture flourished, and which was also the departure point for the annual pilgrimage to Mecca.

When the founding father began giving classes at the mosque, which he had helped to design, the people discovered the breadth of his knowledge and preternatural ability to convey it to his students and disciples. The tribe that had welcomed him wanted to reward him, but he refused to accept any gift in exchange for the diffusion of knowledge – except, dear God, a piece of land where he dug a well. On that plot and around that well, he founded his academy, which graduated dozens of students. At that point, his cousins flocked to him in groups or individually to form the nucleus of a small tribe, which would grow over time, bringing with it a part of the spirit and cultural identity of Chinguetti.

Thus, Nabaa remained simply a place name, around which the tribe and its herds revolved. The herds watered themselves in its valleys when the rains fell. Its core would swell with the cold winds coming from the ocean, and the herds would pasture on its land when the herbage grew.

This new land, the kernel upon which to settle his family with a new tribal identity, was far from Chinguetti and the conflicts of sibling enemies. It needed divine blessing to impart it with holiness, like Chinguetti, which has been described as the seventh most holy city in Islam. That happened when one of the judge's sons came back from the pilgrimage to Mecca. On his journey, he had had to face illness, bandits and jackals, but he had kept a small flask of Zamzam water safe so as to be able to pour it into Nabaa's well, making its blessings endure there forever.

The folk of Nabaa told each other that because of the *baraka* running in its water, there were many "touched" people, and hence frequent cases of emigration. Because of the water, whose power exposed chinks in the soul, many people disappeared on journeys and never came back. The traces of some were lost forever, while many others were found decades later in various places of exile, like birds that had migrated and laid their eggs in some empty place so as to sever any connection with what might come.

* * *

I haven't retained many memories of my childhood. I was perhaps too scatterbrained, too lost in open spaces not crossed by human beings. As a child, I longed to catch a rattlesnake. My dream was to make it my companion along a path replete with dangers. I was going to put it in my room to keep me company, so I might feel its smooth, poisonous skin, and take it with me as I headed ceaselessly towards the sunset in pursuit of the red disc, only arriving after a journey of a month or more at the ocean, the Atlantic Ocean. I had only one objective: to see the swashing of the sea and hear the ceaseless roaring of the waves. The roaring would not stop, and I would not stop enjoying it. I also longed to come across a baby bird of paradise to be my closest friend. Like the prophet Solomon, I would talk to it, and it would talk to me. It would reveal mysteries and I would tell it my woes. Because none of that happened except in my imagination, I instead collected harmless lizards when I came across them in holes in the dry wadi, or when they reared up on their hind legs to sniff the

breeze and I knew they were extracting the secret mois-
ture. For that reason, I longed to be like them. To begin
with I hung them from my shoulder, their tails tied together. I felt so proud of myself, the world wasn't big
enough to contain my feeling of superiority. In the end,
however, I put them in a wooden box with a drawer,
just to watch their colours change from the reddish gold
of the soil into the green of the spiny plants and the deep
blue of the sea. Yes, rattlesnake, bird of paradise, sea,
lizards, waves and gold mixing with the colour of the
sea made up my childhood, a childhood of few games
and much running after camels, goats, dogs and everything else that ran, walked or crawled over the earth.
Running, sprinting, racing and urgently following a target that never went out of sight, even if I shut my eyes.
The only exception was the butterflies, which I did not
chase to catch, because butterflies were rare in the central
Sahara. I might only have seen one once or twice, but
each time something funny and unexpected happened.
What with all the distances I covered, flitting here and
there like a young bird without wings, I saw plenty of
faces, veiled and exposed, but in the end just a few incidents and characters have remained in my memory.
Their images haunt me. They pass across my mind,
blurred and distorted, like the remnants of dreams. Faces
I know and which know me. Some kept me company
for a short time: the time it took to escape the ties of the
memory of a naughty childhood. Others will remain
with me all my life long and are clearly delineated, sep-

arate from yet others that appear to me as if emerging from the recesses of some mysterious place.

Among those faces, I remember Abdel Hadi, who was nicknamed al-Majdhoub: the touched man. He was one of those who left an unforgettable impression on me. The man turned from a happy-go-lucky, sociable character into someone lost and severely withdrawn, who indicated his wants with signs. If he did speak, it would be in a whisper. He would go without sleep for days at a time, staying awake praying, dancing, reciting the Qur'an and singing poetry. That state might last for weeks before he returned to his original condition.

The months of Ramadan and Rabi' al-Awwal were particularly bad. He would sing beautiful poetry at religious occasions like the Prophet's Birthday or the Night of Power on the twenty-seventh of Ramadan. At such times, al-Majdhoub would transition smoothly from al-Busayri's poem rhyming in *meem*, to his poem in *hamza*, to Ibn Farid's poem in *taa*, to the panegyric odes by his grandfather, of which there were many and all of which he knew by heart. His singing of poems would be interspersed with dances of disparate length. His dance floor might be the mosque courtyard or a session for Qur'anic interpretation or lessons in the biography of the prophet, or even a *dhikr* ceremony with one of the Sufi sheikhs.

No one could provide a convincing reason or scientific explanation for why Abdel Hadi's personality changed. He wasn't mad exactly, or ill as, apart from his bouts, he was always compos mentis, and acted normally like most of the community. He managed the affairs of his house to some extent and taught younger children Qur'an and older ones Arabic language and Islamic law.

Abdel Hadi, the touched man, was a rare bird. He had memorised almost the entire corpus of pre-Islamic poetry as well as the collections of Abu Tamam, al-Buhturi, al-Farazdaq, al-Mutanabbi, and many other Umayyad and Abbasid poets.

He had also memorised many works of Maliki jurisprudence and he taught them to his students, particularly the book *The Abridgement of Sheikh Khalil*, with its very copious interpretations and marginalia. In the same vein, he had an encyclopaedic knowledge of the history and genealogy of the Arabs as well as total command of grammar and stylistics, which he also taught in his spacious courtyard. All that diverse and copious knowledge of history, jurisprudence, linguistics and stylistics was of little use, however, when it came to giving the Friday sermon, since against convention, he gave his sermon in the vernacular. This made the children giggle, which drove Abdel Hadi into a rage and from the mosque's pulpit he threatened them with dreadful punishments.

Abdel Hadi, al-Majdhoub, was my master and teacher. He taught me to memorise the *hizbs* of the Holy Qur'an and made the mysterious beauty of the pre-Islamic odes comprehensible. More importantly, his unruly emotional excess slipped into my soul. I am still seized by states of spiritual joy when I hear the chanting of a verse from the Holy Qur'an, or a line of sublime poetry, or when I see a woman's beautiful face. I start dancing like a Naqshbandi dervish at the *hadra* of his master, or like an iridescent bird in a lyrical garden.

Al-Majdhoub imparted some part of his secret to my life. I would be possessed by sublime states like those which possessed him. It happened again and again during my stays and peregrinations in the cities of Kuwait, Doha, Madrid and Dakar, and even in London and New York. I always tried to be the embodiment of his spirituality and wished that he would possess me entirely, along the lines of reincarnation. And to some extent I think those wishes came true.

In his sermons and preaching, al-Majdhoub taught me that money isn't everything. So I forgot the deceit of my friend who promised me a handsome profit on that portion of my salary I gave him for a decade. I was certain that losing the money would not affect me, and so al-Majdhoub's lessons are still there in my mind, opening my eyes to the many blessings God bestows to his worshippers. In that respect I am like my sheikh, taking a good omen from the rain when it waters the thirsty sands. I like to compare the rain that fell in sheets in Madrid, washing the streets and spreading depression and annoyance, with the rain that waters the desolate Saharan lands. Then I might think of dancing with joy as al-Majdhoub did, in gratitude for God's blessings. He had his way, which was my way, too.

To this very day I do not know the secret of the connection between the construction of the mosque and the heavy rains that came after. I believe in fate, and know that God gave the rain to these arid pasturelands following the months of drought. The animals drank and the children swam in pools of water and mud. Then what happened? The first herbage sprouted, splitting the hardness of the parched ground, and a pure miracle appeared before our eyes.

Apart from teaching me to memorise poetry and to choose moments of delight in which to read it, my sheikh al-Majdhoub also taught me to see beauty in the vastness of nature and the desert, which would be carpeted in green after God sent down water and every kind of plant sprouted and grew. He also taught me to see beauty in the faces of enchanting women, who represent the power of seduction in a shoreless sea of temptation.

My Life as Travelogue

My life is a travelogue with countless chapters, each of which has a distinct colour and smell, and a taste anywhere between sweet and bitter. Because of these differences, each chapter curtails and erases what comes before, and engenders what follows in some unforeseen way. It is as if our unknown fate has been eternally written on our wrinkled brows and that which the eye sees, which makes the heart quicken and the tongue speak, is only one of its many manifestations and possible signs.

Of course, I did not expect the letters of the alphabet, about whose mysteries I read in books of magic and fortune telling, would have such a decisive effect on my fate and the fates of those around me. Yet that is what actually happened. My residency in Madrid came to an end with a small news item concerning the Ministry of Finance's list of staff transfers.

The news appeared in *al-Sha'b*, the country's only newspaper at that time. Tucked away and almost invisible, the report was like a jinni taking possession of me and leading me through the labyrinth of life.

I took the news on board with indifference, and calmly waited for what would happen next. I thought that tomorrow would open the gates of a new city to me and I would throw myself into life there. I would forget Spain and my group of friends there, despite all the enjoyable chaos they had caused and all the peccadillos they had committed in good faith. I would no doubt find consolation among new friends with a different lifestyle. Whether I wanted it or not, all that would certainly turn my life upside down.

My new destination was the city of Kuwait, a city that seemed dreadfully boring. At least that's how it seemed at first glance as I made my way from the airport to my residence. At that time, as an astonished new arrival, I discovered that the city was an artificial hybrid trying to cover up its desert identity, but failing to be modern and civilised. A crow imitating the footsteps of a dove. I went on, however, to discover a different flavour to its inhabitants' ways. All that development, the stone, the dust and the sheet glass windows disguised an artificial world that did not reflect the city's reality. What did reflect its authentic truth was the language of the people, their feelings and aspirations.

My appraisal had been right, and thanks to conversations with new friends I soon found myself in the beating heart of the city, and engaged in the details of its heated political life, even though I had never been interested in politics.

Kuwait City seemed the antithesis of Madrid. Here life's spontaneity was negated and we all entered a pre-packaged existence. The dark stale air itself induced depression. Air-conditioning units droned twenty-four seven. Food tasted of the sand stuck in the throat or between the teeth. Taking a walk for a breath of fresh air or sitting in a café opening onto the street were impossible dreams. Yet the beauty of coincidence made life tolerable in Kuwait City after it threw Abdurrahman in my path.

It's hard to confine a human being within a rigid, all-encompassing definition. Abdurrahman and I were born in the same community and brewed in the same pot by fate, yet the outcome for each of us had been very different, and were it not for the twists of fate we would never have met on life's path.

Yes, my life had turned out the opposite of Abdur-rahman's, but we were both rebellious romantics who had grown up quickly. Perhaps it was our longing for independence that united us. However, while Abdurrahman would draw close to a burning flame, I would keep my distance. We were not alike. I always imagined him rather like a dry plant in the desert, easily consumed by fire, while I, according to Abdurrahman, was like a wicker branch in its flexibility and adaptability.

The reason for the difference in our characters was perhaps due to our upbringing. I left the village early and freed myself from the authority of the family to strike out on my own.

In terms of outer appearances, I had learned modern languages and accountancy and found employment at the Finance Ministry, but at heart I had the personality of an ascetic seeking salvation. Sometimes I found that salvation in a Sufism, at peace with the pleasures and joys of life, and at other times by looking inwards and listening, especially when music would inspire me and take me to the abodes of the ascetic mystics. Abdurrahman, on the other hand, had been sent by his family to a Qur'an teacher from a very young age. And what a teacher that teacher was.

When I felt bored in Kuwait, I would go to the Teachers' College accommodation. I would park the Mercedes, flying the national flag – for the benefit of the ambassador, although what's the difference between ambassador and accountant if their joint task is to fiddle the books!

At times the scene there was surreal, but on attending Abdurrahman's circle everything was tolerable, especially when he hosted a pleasant evening around glasses of authentic, dark tea, whose preparation he supervised himself. These sessions were garlanded with his great stories and jokes that revealed his character. He also commented on recent historical events in his own indomitable way: the history of the village, the ocean, the country and the people. But everything began with the village, and to the village returned.

During those sessions, Abdurrahman disclosed to me

his harsh experience under the authority of his first and
last teacher, whom he sometimes enjoyed comparing to
Socrates, the philosopher who liked to generate ideas
and meanings through irony. In some way
Abdurrahman resembled his teacher, even though their
biographies were quite different. To explain the points
of similarity and difference, Abdurrahman said to me:
"My teacher Rajab did not seek wisdom by asking awkward questions, whereas Socrates drank poison for
wisdom's sake. For that reason, perhaps I feel that the fire
of questioning is always aflame on my tongue, and that
I am atoning for the mistakes of my teacher Rajab."

Abdurrahman would often tell me his exciting life
story: he would go over it again and again on different
occasions with different emphases and formulations,
adding new material each time according to his mood
and whatever funny stories, digressions, and allusions
occurred to him. This would drive me into unstoppable
fits of hysterical laughter, by means of which I would
rediscover myself and understand the mysterious aspects
of the many others who had lived in Nabaa and among
its people. They were not the elite or powerful, or part
of the mosque crowd, and in fact often clashed with all
of those. Nonetheless, they left a mark on the community, and when they departed they left behind a void
greater than the space they had occupied in life.

* * *

In the 1970s and '80s, Kuwait was heaving with every idea and militant vision known to the Arab world. Perhaps it was oil and the spread of shy ideas about democracy that had created an ideal environment for a free and diverse press. The presence of thousands of Palestinians given refuge by Kuwait further served to diversify views and pose radical questions, while constant visits by the Palestinian leadership helped to influence the nascent elite and public opinion, eager for what was new. In that atmosphere, Abdurrahman became acquainted with Abu Iyad, who gave him a copy of the book written about him by the French diplomat and journalist Eric Rouleau: *My Home, My Land: A Narrative of the Palestinian Struggle*, in praise of his political experience. At the time Abdurrahman embraced the ideas of the Popular Front for the Liberation of Palestine and listened to the heroic exploits of Wadie Haddad. His revolutionary passion kept burning in the face of rotten reactionaries, as he put it.

I did not have any connection with that milieu. It was hard to know the difference between the PLO, PFLP, and DFLP, just as I was ignorant of the difference between capitalism and socialism. Abdurrahman, however, was the intermediary who taught me all those distinctions and illuminated the shadows between them, as well as teaching me something of Palestinian history and its complications, by comparing and contrasting it with what I did know from our simple shared background as children in the Sahara.

Once, as he was trying to give me an idea of some of the PLO leadership, Abdurrahman said to me that Abu Iyad was like Abdussamad, a diminutive trader from Nabaa, while Abu Saeed (Khaled al-Hassan) was like Salem, a tall, well-built camel herder. Abu Jihad, meanwhile, was like Dahan, the only cloth merchant in the village, whose face bore a permanent sheen of sadness.

Names and scenes came thick and fast from Abdurrahman. At any moment while he was recounting the history of the Palestinian cause, the original names and personalities might blend with those of their counterparts from Nabaa. In this way, the names became familiar and beloved, always testing our confused emotions.

In these late-night story sessions, Abdurrahman also mentioned other names I'd not heard before. Bou Jabara, his Palestinian friend who, according to him, had carried out the first guerrilla operation; Khaled al-Mahnez, an emir from the Gulf renowned for wearing a pungent cologne that Abdurrahman couldn't stand. Others included Leila Khaled, Wadie Haddad, Abu Nidal, Carlos – yes, Carlos – described as a global militant who had sacrificed his life for the Palestinian cause.

When the Sudanese government extradited him to France (more than twenty years later), Abdurrahman was furious, and said the "pimping traitors" had once again shown their malignant political character, their organic ties to global imperialism, and their betrayal of ethical values, the revolution and justice. He predicted their downfall, since the Arab peoples would sweep them away like garbage, and history would sentence them to death.

Abdurrahman was a voracious reader. He loved reading so much that he was addicted. I was mindful of that and brought him back books from every trip I made. He would look over them with the greatest longing, then spend days away from us, holed up reading. I, on the other hand, hated reading, but as if to compensate, I loved Sufi poetry and the rhythms of music. I would be seized by fits of dance and song when I came across poetry and songs that delighted me. Then my heart would find reassurance and I would melt with emotion.

He was a student living in halls. I was an accountant with power and influence at the embassy, especially when the ambassador was absent – and he was away a lot. Were it not for the chemistry between us, Abdurrahman and I would not have met, nor been drawn to each other to form along with others a group that never split up, despite differences in age and interests.

* * *

The 1991 Gulf War brought many changes. First, Kuwait lost part of its spirit. The press was no longer as free and became obsessed with who was for, and who was against. Still, I understood the exceptional circumstances.

The situation imposed on the Kuwaitis had devastating effects. The oil wells that were set on fire brought part of life of this Arab country to an end. Its people turned against a nationalism that promoted war and destruction. That was my view and also that of Abdurrahman. For the first time we shared the same opinion about a complex situation that was difficult to reduce to a few words or simple emotions.

Usually we disagreed about everything. I had stood on the side of Iraq, while Abdurrahman loved Iran and was infatuated with Imam Khomeini to the point of sanctifying him. I was on the right of the political spectrum, while with his rosy romantic ideas and sentiments he always leaned left.

He had lived through the history of national struggle as part of "The Toilers' Movement" when he was still a teenager. He painted walls red with slogans against the regime and distributed the clandestine publication *The Cry of the Oppressed,* which was the mouthpiece of the Toilers. He applauded the lawyer and singer Mohammed Sheen for his famous song "Lend a Hand to the Toilers", which was all the rage among students.

Without Abdurrahman, my life would have been meaningless. Through him I learnt the meaning of difference, acceptance of others' opinions and respect for those holding them, even if they were wrong. When it came to football matches, we agreed to support opposite teams. That was our way of enjoying the game, but also our way of life.

57

His room at the university halls of residence acted as a bookshop, café, and first-rate cultural club. He would wear his baggy desert robe and crouch in front of his teamaking equipment, while everyone else hovered around him. Mauritanian and Arab students made up part of his circle, which also included Africans and Asians. He would pour them strong tea and pour scorn on ideas he did not like, calling their advocates by his favourite expression "dim reactionaries".

Nobody got annoyed with his harsh comments, and his friend the Kuwaiti student, scion of a rich family, who was a permanent presence at his sessions, even confided in me one day that he expected the young Mauritanian man would one day become a leader of the global rebellion.

* * *

After Kuwait, Doha, in Qatar. And Doha then wasn't like it is today, a city of towers competing with Dubai, which has been building upwards for a long time. Back then its architecture was basic, but it hosted a rich cultural life. Many Arab authors and intellectuals from Egypt, Syria and Sudan had emigrated there to work as teachers or government employees.

I still remember al-Wasila, a meek Sudanese gentleman whom Abdurrahman nicknamed Ubeid after a man from Nabaa who was like him. Al-Wasila worked in a government department in Doha, but he was an ascetic by nature, with Sufi tendencies, and often chanted the poetry of chaste and mystical love, of which he had memorised many verses. He and Abdurrahman became firm friends.

Al-Wasila once had the chance to buy a cheap car. He went ahead and bought it to drive to Saudi Arabia and perform the Hajj pilgrimage. Abdurrahman, however, warned him against driving the car, telling him: "Mister Ubeid, don't drive yourself. You're only good for intoning sublime poetry." Al-Wasila laughed and paid no attention to this advice.

A day after his departure, we heard that he had died, crushed by a lorry driven by a drunken Filipino.

The mourning session for al-Wasila was a notable event. We all assembled to recite prayers and invoke the sweet voice of the deceased, which had deafened us as he swayed right and left in his white turban. His voice penetrated the veils of souls when he sang the *ta'iyyah* of Ibn al-Farid.

Such was the Doha through whose alleyways Abdurrahman led me. One of his unique characteristics was the creation of worlds whose entrances only he knew. He resolved contradictions, bringing a Sudanese writer and a Kuwaiti student from a rich family together with a Mauritanian diplomat and destitute Somali students. When we went our separate ways, each would go back to his own world until the next time we got together and the chemistry was there again – as if we had been acquainted since the dawn of creation.

In Doha, Abdurrahman got to know many Sudanese and attended their get-togethers. He listened to their music, with its five-tone scale and Sufi poetry. When I attended one of those sessions with him, I came across Ibrahim al-Shoush, the editor of *Doha* magazine, along with the novelist Tayeb Salih. I danced with them to the rhythms of Sudanese music as we listened in delight to the Sudanese singer Abdulkarim al-Kabili, who sang in a voice charged with sadness the poem by al-Boraei that starts:

Leave passion to a lover whose tears are his lifeblood
Memory confuses him and makes him nothing

going as far as:

Mohammed, lord of lords, from Mudar
Secret of the Prophets, reviver of religion, his
excellence
Unique in majesty, unique in goodness, his glory
Unique in existence, purest of heart, most
merciful
Justice his path, virtue his nature
Dread precedes him, victory serves him.

Tears overwhelmed the singer. He burst out crying and we wept with him.

* * *

Tayeb Salih gave Abdurrahman a copy of his novel

Season of Migration to the North. Abdurrahman was delighted and read it with great passion. Then he began summarising it to me in his singular relational style, whereby he gave each of the novel's characters the name of someone similar from the village of Nabaa. Like that, he made the novel accessible to me without my needing to read it, which was good since I lacked the patience to read more than three pages of any book.

He told me that the novel's protagonist, Mustafa Saeed, was none other than the son of our village, al-Bahi Mohamed, as he was known, or Abah Ould Mohamed Hurma Nineh, as we called him. The only difference between them was that Mustafa Saeed was a ladies' man, while al-Bahi was a militant who had gone into exile and become a leader of the left in Morocco. "Imagine," continued Abdurrahman in his rapid rhythm, "how on earth al-Bahi, who lives in Paris and has written a book describing it, could come back and live in our Saharan town without discarding his Parisian habits."

What if al-Bahi, who had immersed himself in Parisian life and imbibed the ideas of the French enlightenment, had returned to Nabaa, married a conservative woman and spent his days with his old friends drinking tea and performing *dhikr* at the mosque! What kind of character would he be then? A person from Nabaa on the outside, and from Paris on the inside. How dramatic to house such a contradiction, such tension.

I found the comparison amusing as I thought about those old men who had retired early and whose lives remained confined between long sessions drinking green tea and chewing over stories of their past, and watching the herds of goats returning from their pastures at the end of the day.

Their evenings, which lasted throughout the night hours, comprised *dhikr*, poetry and impromptu competitions, as well as sessions of prayer. It seemed they had no taste for sleep. Where, then, was the place of their Parisian companion who had left them and for whom fate would write a different history? Did they still remember the poetry collection al-Bahi had penned before he absented himself? Did they still talk about him as if he were a character from the *1001 Nights*?

Our conversation about al-Bahi took on added impetus after Abdurrahman met him by chance on holiday in Paris. They arranged to meet at a small café in the Latin Quarter. Al-Bahi arrived carrying a copy of *Le Monde* and ordered his coffee black from the waiter whom he addressed by name. They seemed on very friendly terms.

At the time, Abdurrahman showered him with questions about his past, especially his migration from Nabaa in the footsteps of his maternal uncle, the leader Harama Ould Babana: an amazing giant of a man who set the world on fire the day he set off as a freedom fighter to expel the French, who had colonised the entire north African region.

"Was the struggle to kick out the coloniser your main reason for emigrating?" Abdurrahman asked him.

Al-Bahi laughed as he swirled his coffee in its demi-tasse and took a sip, relishing the taste that had become familiar since he stopped drinking green tea, which made his head spin and gave him stomach ache.

With a sweeping gesture, al-Bahi gestured to the south of Paris, as if indicating the southern edge of the world nestling inside of him, where Nabaa was situated. "I emigrated for various reasons," he said. "The struggle was one of them, but it was the desire for change that every Bedouin holds that spurred me to leave." Giving a pure smile, he added: "Abdurrahman, the Bedouin spirit lives within us even when we live in Paris. Whenever we change places, we believe we are going somewhere better. But in reality, we always live in our original places. Ultimately, we are prisoners of our being Bedouin. And as you can see, it's a life sentence.

"Migration is one of life's rich experiences, especially if it's a migration we choose. All major historical events are connected to migration: Judaism is linked to migration; Christianity is linked to migration; Islam is linked to migration. Even the revolutions of the modern era are linked to a kind of migration. Lenin migrated to Switzerland. Mao Zedong migrated from the south of China to the north on the long march of eight thousand kilometres. De Gaulle migrated to Britain. Khomeini migrated to France. The examples are many.

"On a personal level, I come from a line of migrants. Our ancestor came from the north as a migrant and we have the 'migration gene' in our DNA. And it's an active gene in me, and in many of my family members and close relatives.

"True, migration means severing the connection with a place and an excessive reliance on memory, but I think that fear of that and the attempt to overcome it were what caused my cousin, Tijani Ould Bab, who migrated at the end of the nineteenth century, to write an account of his travels that ended in Turkey, and caused another cousin, Ahmed ibn al-Amin, to write his book *al-Wasit* in Egypt, all to maintain a strong relationship with a place and keep the embers of memory aglow. I think that is also what will make me write.

"I still remember the names of many places, perhaps because they appeared in poetry, even if I've forgotten where they are on the map. Like Mulayha, for instance:

'Around Mulayha, pitch camp, then awake
    and go, awake and go.'

And like Rukab:

'Halt in Rukab on your mount and greet it
    Bid peace to the site of its encampments
A place, traces in memory, in the heart
    Hidden, its dead of old and its living.'"

Abdurrahman expected his meeting with al-Bahi to last an hour or a little more. Time was precious in Paris and he was not greedy for more, knowing that al-Bahi had many commitments. Nonetheless, al-Bahi cancelled all that day's appointments, because for the first time he felt he was re-evoking the place he had lost since leaving for Senegal in the footsteps of his uncle Harama Ould Babana, and heading by boat from Dakar to Tarfaya, Morocco, on the edge of the Sahara. He recalled it all and talked at length, as if reliving that time again.

The two men moved on to a restaurant, Chez Hamadi, on Rue Boutebrie off Boulevard Saint-Michel. A small place where al-Bahi ate when he wanted to be alone. Then he started to recall the names of his old friends, one by one, comparing his life and fate with those of people he had lost touch with. He seemed to only still recall the features and characteristics that were hardest to forget.

Finally, Abdurrahman said: "They haven't forgotten you and wish you could visit them some day."

Al-Bahi laughed and said: "True, but your military rulers don't wish that and won't allow it. I'll wait till they've gone back to their barracks."

"I hope that will be soon," replied Abdurrahman.

They then embraced and said goodbye.

Al-Bahi went down the marble steps into the Metro station, his copy of *Le Monde* tucked under his arm. He gradually receded into the gloom of a tunnel, some of whose lights were broken, and became part of Paris's unknowable arteries.

Abdurrahman went back to his hotel to wait for his trip to Doha. He stood at the window alone, looking at the Parisian night, studded with lights. In a wave of longing and amazement, he brought to mind the details of that meeting, which would remain etched in his memory.

* * *

When Abdurrahman finished university, his graduation day was a grand event. Along with his friends, he sat waiting in the auditorium to receive his degree certificate. He remained somewhat subdued by the formal atmosphere, and when his name was called, he nervously accepted his certificate and made a quick exit. To explain why he hadn't attended the party, he gave one of his favourite retorts: "I went to get a breath of freedom."

That freedom – Abdurrahman's choice of lifestyle – was curtailed over the months he then spent confined to the army barracks, a time during which his relationship with us and his special world was severed. He no longer met with us to tell his amazing stories, the oral history of the village of Nabaa, nor to narrate the history of the heroic world whose characters, images and events he invoked.

Abdurrahman submitted to hard months of military training in Qatar alongside recruits from the Philippines and Egypt. They taught him to use a gun and to perform checks on substances to determine if they were prohibited.

I expected that during that period he would not be in a position to choose his words or apply his epithets to those he liked. He would not provide the endings to the innumerable stories that had been the highlight of his highly enjoyable gatherings.

Abdurrahman, a policeman in Qatar . . . now that was hard to believe. A tale straight out of a nightmarish imagination, not one accustomed to happy endings. Still, it was part of the unusual personality that formed the events of his life and marked him out from others. That was my opinion, and I defended it vehemently. I was right, and moreover one might say it was I who had determined Abdurrahman's fate. It was I who had suggested he sit the police entrance exam, telling him confidently: "You'll pass easily, given you have a university degree, are highly cultured, and have an amazing ability to make friends." He didn't pay much attention at the time, but the random arrow I shot hit home.

At the time, Mauritania was experiencing a new wave of emigration after the UAE opened its doors to young Mauritanians wishing to join the police force. Thousands went to Abu Dhabi to try their luck, but everyone referred to them as the Qatari police, including those trying for the Emirati police. Recruits would leave their training camps after eleven months of standing in the blazing Gulf sun, which roasted faces and limbs, to work as guards at government offices or to direct traffic at road junctions. Then they would go back home, spend their savings in a month, get married at lavish ceremonies to women whose blood flowed with adventure, and in the end return, empty-handed and heavily in debt, and perhaps divorced from their wives.

When Abdurrahman recounted his short experience in the real Qatar police, he refused to admit he was a policeman, but tended to describe his job as a mix between a public scrivener (as per the novels of Tahar Ben Jelloun) and a customs officer in high-tech Japanese style.

Nobody actually knew what Abdurrahman really did, and when he tendered his resignation, it was a shock to all. He later told us excerpts from the story, but as digressions punctuating various other interwoven stories.

We did subsequently learn that he had been tasked with manning the scanner checking shipments at the border. He also took on the task of composing begging letters for his less well-educated colleagues, asking for assistance or promotion, which in his own way did make him a public scrivener.

Abdurrahman wasn't comfortable with his job as a policeman. Most of his salary went on meeting the requests of family and friends living a consumerist lifestyle. The letters he received from them would enclose cuttings from *Sayidati* magazine showing pictures of French perfumes and Swiss watches. Satisfying the requests of friends was an obligation in Abdurrahman's moral code, so when he left the Gulf to start a new life full of contradictions and holes, he was empty-handed and in debt.

Rajab's Shade-Giving Tent

Rajab, as described by Abdurrahman, was thin, dark-skinned and of medium stature. His face was scarred, perhaps the traces of some fight that nobody knew about, although the man was docile and wouldn't hurt a fly. I wondered who would have dared mark him with deep wounds to the face.

Living alone in his own unique form of solitude, Rajab refused to be part of the system that defined the mutual life of the village. His original act of rebellion was against the iniquitous rites of marriage. But that was only the first red banner of protest he raised against inherited conventions, protests which over time became non-negotiable.

Rajab refused to contemplate marriage, satisfied with loving whichever daughter of Eve he wished. He liked plump girls, who caused him to melt with love, and would give forceful expression to his feelings, contrary to other men who cloaked themselves in a dishonest silence. He had actually been married once, to a daughter of Eve from a town far from Nabaa. He spent one night with his wife, then extricated himself. He understood that all the restrictions delineating family life did not suit his rebellious temperament and were not for him.

Rajab's shade-giving tent was pitched between the houses. His cows, which he did not allow anyone else to look after, milled around the tent, which was home, shelter and refuge. He was part of it, as if he were the pegs and poles holding it up. The tent was also the *kuttab* and school, filled with boys to whose education Rajab had dedicated his life. In the end, the tent became a Nabaa landmark.

Rajab was not content with just teaching the boys. He domesticated them, giving them his cows' milk to drink, feeding them his own food, and generally treating them with boundless generosity. It was for that reason Abdurrahman had stuck to a daily routine with his teacher throughout his youth. The pair of them would walk dozens of miles together in the surrounding desert wilderness, committing the Holy Qur'an to memory along with whatever was possible from the poetry of Ghaylan Dhu al-Rumma, before they arrived at the locality of the woman Abdurrahman had fallen head over heels in love with at the height of his youthful prowess.

On the way back from those lengthy excursions, they would stop at a lone *sarh* tree standing between the sand dunes. Rajab would lie down beneath it for a short rest before they resumed the path to Nabaa. He would hang his transistor radio from one of the branches to listen to the musical pieces Radio Mauritania broadcast before the one o'clock news bulletin. When the presenter announced it was precisely one o'clock and began reading the news, the teacher's face would darken and he would curse the family tree of the newsreader, who had interrupted the beautiful melodies to talk about world events in which Rajab had not the slightest interest.

"This is Nouakchott," the presenter would say.

Rajab would get angry and say: "These are the groves outside Nabaa. This is a *sarh* tree. Nouakchott is miles away, you little liar!"

Rajab had no difficulties in contacting his girlfriends. Equally, his girlfriends had no qualms about sitting and talking to him. All the local women, and many of the men, knew that Rajab's relationships with women were chaste and did not transgress any religious sensibilities, confined as they were to some verbal flirtation which might include the odd rude word, but which only added a little spice and humour to the conversation. Overall, however, his dalliances remained socially and religiously acceptable.

When Rajab fell for a woman, he would usually ask her for a piece of her underwear or to show him the henna patterns on her hands, but in the end he would be content with giving a chuckle and heading off, followed by his pupils chanting the Qur'an without much reverence.

I did hear that Rajab had become a partner in a commercial venture, the first of its kind in the village. The idea was to set up a business to supply the village with foodstuffs and other things to meet demand. Rajab paid the value of seven cows for a significant number of shares in the new enterprise.

The commercial establishment turned into the centre of village life, a place where the nomadic Bedouin who sought pasture in the neighbouring area would come to purchase essentials. At the same time the place began to play other roles. It served as a hotel to host travellers, except that it provided the service for free. It was also a café which served hot tea free of charge, and was the meeting place for the Society of Those Qualified to Bind and Unbind, which was an influential group from the mosque. All of the society's historic decisions concerning the village were taken there.

Rajab observed the growth of the shop and the interest in it. He did not, however, internalise the first lesson of the law of capital, namely to make a profit and accumulate a surplus. By nature, he tended towards socialism without clearly understanding what it meant.

Because the whole population of Nabaa knew that Rajab the teacher owned a considerable number of shares in the new emporium, those who knew how generous he was took the opportunity to exploit this fully. As usual, they persistently aired their needs to him, while he had only one response: to meet those needs at once and with good grace.

Over time, Rajab's debts accumulated until he found himself out of the company and no longer a shareholder, having sold his shares to pay off seemingly infinite debts.

For the children, Rajab's behaviour provided their first lesson in socialism, and in siding with the weak. Abdurrahman learnt that lesson from his teacher, as he told us, and we imbibed it too. We talked about it during long nights spent reminiscing over the traits and glorious feats of Rajab the teacher.

Rajab's most important lesson, however, lay in his ability to pass on his refined taste in poetry and music to his listeners and those close to him. That left a significant impression on our lives. He left behind him a rare imprint on our hearts, crowning all that with a rare lack of interest in money, a quality to be found only among the great Sufis.

Three Men and a Woman

Fortunately, my posting in Qatar came to an end for I did not much relish the prospect of being a prisoner in my apartment once Abdurrahman had left Doha in revolt at the restriction to his freedom. The beautiful world he had created disappeared with him. So, I too packed my bags, and requested a transfer to another embassy. This turned out to be none other than our embassy in Guinea, which diplomats usually avoided like the plague, using every trick and connection, and going as far as bribing the minister or giving a gift to the first lady to ensure they would be reassigned. I, however, was willing to do all that and more just to be sent there!

I don't know why or when I was seized by the idea of going to Guinea and leaving behind the Gulf, that chimera of wealth and money. I do remember, though, that Abdurrahman was the only person who encouraged the idea, which he described as a stroke of genius when I told him about it. In fact, he provided me with a few arguments that I was lacking in order to defend the idea, not just to other people but also to myself. I found those justifications reasonable and endorsed them.

The first argument Abdurrahman supplied that struck a chord with me was that life in Conakry would be completely different from anything I had known before. Not a raucous life atop a nightclub, like in Madrid, and certainly not the monotonous air-conditioned life in sealed rooms like in the Gulf. It would be a new life experience, a taste of adventure and the pleasure of discovery, as if I were being reborn.

Abdurrahman's second argument concerned the hue and cry that Mariam the fortune teller had caused recently when she told us that three of our lost cousins were still alive, albeit speaking in strange accents. These three men had emigrated to Guinea from Nabaa many decades earlier. News of them had dried up and nobody knew where they were. Finding them or discovering their fate would have great significance for the community of Nabaa, unrivalled, as a laughing Abdurrahman put it, by anything but the discovery of the source of the Nile or the deciphering of the Rosetta Stone.

Mariam the Cowrie Shell Reader

Mariam was highly respected within the community and enjoyed a seldom-found spiritual authority among the men of Nabaa as well as the women. This was in fact due to her other-worldly ability to act as a bridge between the world of the dead and the world of the living, with a kind of trunk line for sending spoken messages and exchanging news and information.

From Nabaa and beyond, people flocked to Mariam's tent. Some came seeking news of relatives who had left this world: How had they been received in the limbo of Barzakh, and were they happy? Others came in search of kin, long lost in the mazes of the Sahara and about whom reports conflicted: Had they died from thirst as some said and had Mariam met them in the after world? A third group came to ask Mariam to send greetings to their intellectual or spiritual masters who had departed for the other world. Also not absent from the crowds were those who came to make fun of her, denying what she said and belittling what she did.

Mariam welcomed the arrivals and answered their questions one by one from behind a curtain. For the most part they went away pleased with what she had told them about the fates of their relatives, perhaps giving them verbal messages or advice from the dead, which contained accurate details about personal incidents only they would know. Sometimes Mariam would apologise and not give an answer about the fate of a specific person, claiming she had not seen them in the limbo of Barzakh or had not recognised them. That left room for malign tongues to wag.

To obtain this information or answer these questions, Mariam only had to take a five-minute nap, but she woke up anxious and confused, as if coming out of a prolonged epileptic fit.

Mariam's job as postman between the living and the dead was impossible to keep separate from the story of her own miraculous survival. She had been lost in the waterless desert for more than a week and reunited with her family, or rather her family reunited with her, many years later.

I was not alive at the time, as I was born twenty or thirty years after the event, but I had heard Mariam's story – or more accurately the story of the person believed to be Mariam – many times. Everyone was aware of it, with slight variations, and I took pride in it as one of the miracles that constituted Nabaa.

The event had unfolded during one of the droughts that afflicted the country. The community had set off in search of pasture for their few herds. The young Mariam had climbed out of her mother's *howdah* to relieve herself during a violent sandstorm, which had resulted in the tribe dispersing. Her mother, on the camel, was transported a long way off and then deposited on the ground. When she retraced her steps to look for her daughter, she found no sign of her.

The girl's family spent months searching for her, but could find no trace and heard no word. When they lost hope and became certain she must have died, they held a funeral in her absence, then sank into silent submission to fate. However, her mother, who was considered a pious woman, never lost hope of her daughter's return and said she would come back one day.

The very day that Mariam became separated from the caravan, she was found by a salt-trading caravan that was roaming the region. They took her with them, and their chief adopted her, as Mariam related many years later to her elderly mother, her friends and the women of the community. Each time Mariam told her story she added a few details, but she was always consistent and unstinting in her praise of the family who had adopted her and who never made her feel she was an orphan or a stranger.

That family spent years looking for the little girl's relatives without success until a report reached one of Nabaa's leading men. He sent a delegation of men and women to find out about the girl. The day she returned to Nabaa was remarkable, its joy only tempered by the whispers of a few women who claimed they could not see the traces of the deep wound on her forehead that had previously been visible, nor the white birthmark that had been on her chest since the day she was born.

Mariam's life was enigmatic, since apart from the riddle of her identity, which was never completely cleared up and remained a matter of doubt for some, her behaviour was alien to the Nabaa community. She did not eat meat, spoke in tongues during her sleep, talked about invisible things, and claimed to communicate with the jinn.

The day after her return to Nabaa, she had begun to give reports of the unseen world. Occasionally her prophecies would be proven right, but for the most part she would find some justification to give vague, ambiguous interpretations which left her questioners perplexed.

Mariam's prophecies about the three cousins who had been lost opened the door of hope to the people of Nabaa. Like her, they had vanished without trace, but had she not returned after being lost in the desert? So, wondered their relatives, might they too not come back one day, even if only in blurred dreams?

Whenever Mariam talked about the return of the lost men, she would provoke the ire of many of those who considered them among the dead. Her fiercest critic was al-Majdhoub, who once said to her with startling boldness: "Mariam, your father was not a wicked man and your mother was not a whore. What you are doing is neither your family's occupation nor the *sunnah* of your prophet. No, it is the work of Shaitan, the Devil. I warn you not to be like one of the people of Jahiliya, that time of ignorance before the Prophet Mohammed. Leave off reading cowrie shells, divining with sand and inquiring into the unseen. Knowledge of the unseen is for God alone and no one with a whit of reason or religion would believe what you see. Repent and seek forgiveness from God."

However, I was the opposite of my touched sheikh al-Majdhoub and believed everything that Mariam said. Since she had spoken of these missing men, I had had a mystifying sense verging on certainty that, just as dawn light emerged from the darkness of night, they would appear again in our world, somewhere in Guinea.

A few days after taking up my post at the embassy in Conakry, I went to see the head of mission and asked his permission to take a few days off for a trip to help clear up one of the severe bouts of asthma that afflicted me from time to time. Then I handed him the cheque book, together with some signed blank cheques. His features lit up when he saw the cheques and he gave his permission at once, advising me to look after my health and to try and get better. He saw me off at the door with a broad grin.

I put on the white African robe I had bought at the market in the city centre and the turban I had inherited from my grandfather. As it was raining – usual for equatorial Conakry, where a single day's rainfall was more than double the amount our country received in a whole year – I also draped a plastic bag over my whole body, as they do here to keep their clothes dry. I walked through the mud and rain in search of a taxi to take me to Labé, capital of the Fouta Djallon in central Guinea.

Since childhood, I had heard about the men who left Nabaa, but knew little of their fate. The stories about them were contradictory: some said they had died, while others related how they were living dull lives in Fouta Djallon. Shortly before I arrived from Doha, I had heard that one of them, Mohammedi, was living in Labé and enjoyed great respect among the Fulani tribes who had settled that city of two hundred thousand souls.

The journey to Labé took seven hours and I arrived a little before sunset. The city was located at some altitude and its air was pleasingly fresh. I went through its beautiful gateway and passed by the grand mosque, absorbed in its interesting details.

It was not difficult to locate the house of the *sherif*: the term here for any Arab. Everybody knew him because he was the imam at the main mosque. He gave the sermon at Eid and was also sheikh of the only Sufi *zawiya* in the city. In addition, he was married to four women.

The *sherif*, who had left Nabaa when I was still very young, knew who I was as soon as I said my father's name. He led me into his own room via a stone-paved corridor bright with colourful flowers and overflowing with lush green plants. Then we turned towards the entrance to the *zawiya* and stood for a while in the large, silent and tranquil room. At the far end of the room, which was almost devoid of furniture, I spotted tea-making equipment on a small wooden shelf carved with an African motif. He sat me down on a wooden bed covered in a zebra skin and sat opposite me, having spread out his prayer mat. He ordered one of his wives, who had appeared in the doorway, to fetch me a bowl of fresh cow's milk, while he began the tea ceremony.

Mohammedi was tall and thin with quite dark skin. His hair had gone white, and although he must have been eighty years old or more, he was still in good health and had the zest for life of a young man. He told one joke after another, although many of them would no longer be thought of as in good taste.

He told me how he had originally travelled to Senegal in search of work in the businesses owned by relatives, but had found travelling from one city to another enjoyable in istelf. He would stay in a city for a while, working as a Qur'an teacher or religious guide, then move onto another. His peregrinations continued until fate landed him in the heart of the jungle.

Mohammedi wiped his brow as he set an empty glass on the copper table that had accompanied him since leaving Nabaa nearly sixty years earlier. His daughter brought in a small tin-plate burner, and he put the *ibriq* on the coals, and launched into a long speech. He praised Labé, extolling the virtues of its inhabitants, and related the history of the notables he had encountered when he arrived, and of Hajj Karamoko Alfa Diallo Labé, the weird and wonderful man who had founded the city in the eighteenth century. He had made it the capital of the Islamic state he established in this forgotten part of Guinea.

Handing me a glass of hot tea, the *sherif* continued his account. Hajj Karamoko had studied in Mali and became one of the leading scholars of his era. A singular leader, he united the entire Fouta Djallon region under his banner. His grave was still a site of pilgrimage behind the grand mosque, which he had built on a hill in his new capital. Leaders, commanders, scholars and politicians (mostly from his clan) would visit it to ask God to have mercy on him, and to draw on his virtues.

The same wife brought the bowl of milk. I drank my fill, then the *sherif* handed me the two remaining glasses of tea, one after the other. The pale light coming in from the balcony that overlooked the dark green canopy signalled the ending of the day, and Sheikh Mohammedi invited me to spend the night as an honoured guest. He led me back to the house where I would sleep. Before he stood up to say goodnight, he turned to me and quoted a line from an old Mauritanian poet: "One who sees not Labé, sees neither world nor man." He said it laughing, then left the room and closed the door behind him.

I wanted to tell the man, who had only seen this limited part of the Fatou Djallon, that life consisted of rivers flowing in various worlds and courses, that their hidden waters flowed through cities spread throughout God's wide world, whose inhabitants might be red, yellow,

white or black, beautiful and refined, or wild and ignorant, and that the world did not begin or end with this
Guinean city.

I did not do that, though, because I did not wish to
break the flow of his thoughts. I had come here to meet
him and listen to him. Perhaps the romance of his life
and his delight in his good fortune had seduced me. The
man was extremely happy, and crowned with esteem
and respect. The whole city – its rocks, its air and its
women, especially his four wives, who competed to fulfil
his desires – was at his service.

Mohammedi did not know that his friends, whom he
had left as an adolescent, had now become renowned
sheikhs with grandchildren, nor that the "tent village"
jostled with buildings, nor that modern schools, to
which families had once been afraid to send their children to study lest it impact on their religion, now had
their doors wide open to all.

Mohammedi seemed a little saddened that he would
never find the world he had left behind, given all those
changes. He felt that going back to his ancestral homeland was impossible, and that the conditions of life in
Labé would not be available in Nabaa, where a man
could only marry one woman, who would pester and
nag him about everything and impose the law of women
which stipulates that a happy marriage is one where the
man does what the woman wants and the woman does
what she wants.

The darkness spread rapidly and cloaked the vague objects around me, transforming them into shadow beings. Thank God for the pale illumination of a lamp. Next, the sheikh's eldest daughter led me back to the *zawiya*, where there was a wooden bed covered with a white sheet. A few books on Sufism lay around it, including Ibn Arabi's *The Meccan Conquests*, Abu Hamid al-Ghazali's *Deliverance from Error*, and Ibn al-Jazari's *The Impregnable Stronghold*, as well as some handwritten poetry collections.

I endeavoured to break up the long night by reading but couldn't concentrate. The sheikh remained awake and I kept hearing his voice as he intoned lengthy recitations from the Qur'an. That reverent prayer seemed to rise from the mysterious flitting shadows cast by the body of the night, occasionally punctuated by the sheikh's murmurings, which would continue, uninterrupted and indifferent to the passage of time, until the first heralds of dawn were heard.

In the middle of the night, a chill wind rattled the half-open wooden door, which only made my insomnia worse. Lost in thought, I wondered why people migrated, how migration shaped their fates, and how the environment affected one's personality. Lying on the wooden bed, I imagined for myself a fate similar to the *sherif*'s. Then I fell asleep, only for that same flood of thoughts to run through my dreams, which were regularly punctuated by the banging of the wooden door that itself became part of those confused dreams.

I dreamt that I was a sheikh in Labé, surrounded by

hundreds of slave girls and women, who competed to fulfil my desires and satisfy theirs. I was their sovereign, like Shahryar, or Haroun al-Rashid among his thousand concubines. All these women were alike except for one, who did not resemble the others, but I did not know her name or who she was.

I was woken by the sun's rays pouring through the window and I belatedly completed the dawn prayer. The *sherif* came bearing fresh bread and a bowl of cow's milk. He sat in front of his copper table and prepared the tea. I watched him as he formed the garland of steaming foam. A series of people, all making tea, came to mind. My father, performing the ritual in the early morning after heating the water on a low flame before going to pray at the mosque. Teresa, sitting cross-legged on the floor like Buddha, pouring the tea from glass to glass to create the white froth on top of the red liquid. And finally, Abdurrahman, surrounded by students on the campus in Doha.

The *sherif* invited me to follow his example, insisting it would be easy for him to marry me to four women before sundown. I found the idea amusing, as if part of my obscure dream had come true. But I thought I ought not to increase the tide of sadness that had washed over Nabaa for decades, during which its sons, one after another had become lost in faraway exile.

I wondered if it was my place to blow on the embers of grief and inflame it with another migration – for the sake of four Guinean women.

I also did not want to spoil the sheikh's enjoyment at his proposal. Not out of politeness, as one might think, but because of his formidable authority and prestige. I just said: "I'm interested and will pray for guidance once I've returned to Nabaa and brought them the good tidings of my trip to Labé."

Before saying goodbye to him, I asked about his two companions in the foreign land of Guinea. Since the three of them had left Nabaa, no one had seen them, and they had sent no news. All that remained were conflicting rumours, which included elements of myth and legend. The people of Nabaa still had doubts, and those who were certain they had died would argue with those who claimed they were still alive.

* * *

Mohammedi sat up straight and his face lit up. For decades he had not had someone to listen to him confess his innermost secrets. He had left behind the friends with whom he shared childhood memories and games so long ago that he had almost lost the ability to tell the story.

For a while, Mohammedi contemplated his palm, as if he wanted to learn the future from its deep lines. Then he spoke: "I've only seen Mohammed al-Hafez on a few occasions. He chose to live in a tiny remote village separated from us by a river and mountains. We did not even reach this country together, although we followed more or less the same path.

"We have both lived among the Fulani: the wonderful tribe that originates from Nubia, and is even said to be descended from the pharaohs. Their women are as tall as palm trees and generally have very fine features. Good company and attractive, they have a feminine ability to hang on to their husbands, whose secret only they know. As is customary when the people here deal with *sherifs*, we were both treated very generously. The tribal elders made us an offer we could not refuse, namely, choosing wives from among the most beautiful girls. It was very tempting, for every woman in Fatou Djallon dreams of marrying an Arab of noble lineage. Yes, I suppose our migration was for a woman to marry and have a share in this world, not for the sake of God as it is written in the *hadith*. That's the indubitable truth, and you can tell that to al-Majdhoub, who will certainly be angry and say that we wasted our lives and lost out in this world and the next. You can also tell Rajab the teacher. Perhaps he'll join us and make up for all the time he's wasted!"

The *sherif* picked up a glass of tea that one of his daughters had brought him, touching it to make sure it was still hot. He took a large mouthful before continuing: "We came with few possessions, but in record time we became major owners of cattle, with plenty of servants. It was like that for me and for Mohammed al-Hafez, but Ould al-Taher has a different story."

Mohammedi adjusted his position and continued his story, struggling to keep it under control. It seemed as if he were completely ignoring me now, only addressing himself, or sending a message to the people of Nabaa through me. That's what he intended, of course, but he was actually talking to the wall in front of him. The mechanics of free association (as in psychoanalysis) pushed him to disclose events in his old life and to try to revive them in his memory again.

His eyes were fixed on a hat hanging on the wall. It was woven from leaves, and was used to keep off the sun and also to cover dishes of food. The dignified man said: "Mohammed al-Hafez's talents were readily evident from the beginning, and he became heavily involved in letter magic, which provides the power to harness the jinn and make them obey. He controlled the jinn and made them do what he wanted. Through them he can even harness the laws of nature, see the future, and make people do his will, like it or not.

"His magical powers were renowned in the region. He cured the chronically ill just by blowing on them. Merchants turned to him when they were robbed by thieves. He would tell them who the culprits were, and they would tell the police, or take justice into their own hands. His real fame, however, was due to how he exposed the marital infidelities of men: a very common occurrence in Guinea. When he appeared and men began to fear scandal, cases of marital infidelity dropped markedly and there were far fewer disputes between married couples. Affection and compassion infused families, all thanks to the *baraka* of Mohammed al-Hafez."

Then he continued, as if apologising for how unbelievable it all was, saying that he had not been able to verify everything he heard, but as a believer he accepted that there were things outside the scope of reason and beyond everything people were used to. He had heard many such things, and some of them he had seen with his own eyes!

"And Ould al-Taher? What's his story?" I asked. The *sherif* put his hand over his mouth to mask a resonant laugh. "He's like the jinn himself!" he said. "They see you from where you can't see them! The man is a master of the vanishing act. He left Nabaa in protest at the meagre amount of water they offered him when they were drinking from a pool that had formed after a rain shower. Eyes blazing in fury, he shouted out his famous words: 'I'm going to a place where drinking water comes out of taps!'"

It occurred to me that Ould al-Taher was, with that protest followed by migration, the first climate change refugee!

As I was getting into the car to take me back where I had come from, the *sherif* told me: "If you see an old Arab man wandering the streets of Kindia, walking with the elegance of a gazelle, you should know that it's Ould al-Taher, for sure. He's unmissable because he stands out from other people in his colouring and appearance. But as soon as he sees you, he'll be off like the wind. He'll vanish in the twinkling of an eye. He lives in his own world, which he doesn't want any outsider, especially his kin, spoiling. If you should come across him by chance, don't let him know your real identity. Tell him you're from Fes. Then he'll relax with you because he loves the inhabitants of that city, which he considers his spiritual home."

Staring intently at me, he continued: "Go to Kindia. It's in the region close to Guinea's border with Sierra Leone. The air there is lovely, and the place is rich because of the diamond mines. Its people conceal their wealth in those small but valuable precious stones. Look for him at the taxi station in the middle of town. You'll be sure to find him there, because he's always roaming aimlessly around the place. He goes where he pleases and spends his time moving between the Guinean merchants' houses. They treat him generously and buy him new clothes and give him cans of clean water. Actually, he refuses to drink any liquid that doesn't come out of a can. He's been like that since he left Nabaa in protest at the shortage of water. If you don't find him in Kindia, he might have gone to one of the surrounding villages. He goes from house to house, where they welcome him, but he doesn't beg.

"The only person around who's friendly with him is my son Saeed. He lives in that border region, and Ould al-Taher visits him sometimes for treatment. My son practises folk medicine and treats illnesses with tropical plants, In difficult cases he turns to spells and "letter magic". He's well known there and highly respected. He's married two women so far and will marry the third next month." The *sherif* laughed. "I don't think of him as Arab. He doesn't speak our language.

"So it is, as you've seen and heard. Now you can report back to the folk of Nabaa. They'll be thirsty to know what you can tell them about the three of us. This country has always been hell for its people, many of whom, especially the Fulani, were led off to death camps under President Ahmed Sékou Touré. But for us God made it tantamount to an eternal paradise and we would never seek an alternative. Here the woman are beautiful, and tall as bamboo poles, nature is as magnificent as paradise, and Arabs are honoured beyond honour."

At that moment, I realised what the Nabaa folk had been unable to understand as they pondered the possible reasons as to why some among them had migrated to Guinea and chosen it as an alternative homeland. I also realised just how integrated the *sherif* was in his little world, and how he saw that life began and ended in Labé.

That was the same feeling I had had, too, when I was in Madrid, and the feeling Abdurrahman had had back in Kuwait and Qatar, when the Left, the revolution and the affairs of the Arab nation were of great interest in the petrostates. And at the time the Gulf was open enough to welcome their brother Arabs from well-watered and desert lands.

Abdurrahman Lays Down His Saddle

Abdurrahman eventually lay down his saddle in Nouakchott. The Gulf era came to an end and, as he frequently said, the spark had gone out. He didn't bring much money back from the Gulf, but his heart was brimming with noble values and humanitarian principles, and he was resolved to side with the weak, to support the oppressed, and to speak and defend the truth, whatever the consequences. He also brought back a great many books and a memory that retained a vast amount of poetry, literature, history and politics, as well as funny stories, and experience of deep relationships with people who ranged from the highly religious to the radical atheist, from the tycoon to the janitor, the dissident to the ruling emir, and from the famous intellectual to the unknown Filipino labourer.

At the disorganised library of the Ecole Nationale d'Administration on the campus of Nouakchott University, Abdurrahman brushed the dust off scores of volumes whose pages had not been turned for decades. He had been appointed as a librarian on one of those stormy days when dark dust clouds obscured all the city's landmarks and whipped up endless blasts of yellow sand, as though the city were retching up its innards and readying itself for a violent coughing fit before darkness fell. Abdurrahman, however, braved his way through those blasts of sand and picked up the keys to the library. Despite everything, he was excited, if slightly pained that his sole task would be to keep an eye on the students and prevent them stealing the books.

Abdurrahman arrived in his loose-fitting blue robe carrying a number of books that he wished to donate to the university library.

He addressed the director in a sarcastic tone: "This is a portion of the knowledge I would love to impart to your library. Perhaps it will be of benefit to one of the idiotic students at your institution. Being recently published books, they have yet to reach Mauritania, unlike the yellow-paged ones on your shelves."

The director's face turned yellow with anger. Abdurrahman's effrontery had surprised him. He squinted at him in an effort to make out his face which was partly covered by his *litham*.

Abdurrahman handed him a folder containing his CV and qualifications, and added in the same sarcastic voice: "I have another degree in history, but it was my degree in library science that caught your attention because, after belittling that discipline and even denying its existence, you find you need specialists in the field . . . Fine, there is no better job than working among books.

Borges, the world's greatest living writer, was in charge of the National Public Library in Buenos Aires, but nobody here has heard of Borges or Buenos Aires, or gives any regard to libraries or books!"

The director took Abdurrahman to the office he would share with a colleague. He shook his hand coldly, then disappeared into the dust.

Over time, that shared office on the ground floor overlooking a courtyard constantly eddying with dust would turn into something akin to a cultural café, which Abdurrahman's friends would frequent every day to drink tea and talk. Abdurrahman would play the role of waiter, making and handing out hot glasses of tea to all those present, including the library janitor and students, who would come by from time to time in search of a book or to ask for a reference.

A matter of a few weeks after Abdurrahman took up his post and the office (or café) became a political and cultural club, it would be visited by many of the capital's intellectuals and politicians. Among them were journalists, lawyers, doctors, poets and writers, all conversing about politics, debating cultural issues and ideas, and – most significantly – listening to Abdurrahman's sayings and anecdotes.

By virtue of having studied in the Arab East, Abdurrahman was very well versed in contemporary Arabic poetry and prose. But he mostly talked about leftist intellectuals and writers, whom he favoured for reasons mainly unconnected to their literary worth. For example, he praised the Yemeni poet al-Baradouni for being a blind leftist who calumniated the capital city of Sanaa, and he extolled Ahmed Fouad Negm for being a poor peasant. He urged students to read the novels of the Chilean Isabel Allende because her uncle was Salvador Allende, the president of Chile killed by Pinochet in a CIA-orchestrated military coup. He was also full of praise for Colombian novelist Gabriel Garcia Marquez because he was a friend of Fidel Castro's. When someone asked him quizzically whether blindness, poverty, kinship and friendship could serve as criteria for literary criticism, Abdurrahman replied with a triumphant smile: "The criteria of criticism are a dictatorship that critics impose on readers, and every reader has the right to set down their own standards. 'You have your criteria, and I have mine. You have your art, and I have mine,' as Gibran said."

The office would be packed with people, especially once the students had heard about the nature and level of the discussions taking place. They flocked there, and Abdurrahman encouraged them, saying: "Knowledge is derived from the mouths of men, not the bellies of books. The sages of ancient Greece learned and taught wisdom through dialogue, not through reading. These debates will sharpen your minds and refine your tastes, and they will be of greater benefit than reading a thousand of the yellowing books on the library's shelves."

Firm friendships developed between Abdurrahman and the students and researchers who came to the office, and who spent more time with him drinking tea and listening to his enjoyable conversation than they did studying or reading. You would see them sitting in a circle around him on chairs that had lost their backrests as he told them his funny, occasionally weird, tales, as if he were a traditional storyteller in one of the coffeehouses of old Damascus.

The director had not been a fan of Abdurrahman's since the stormy day they met when he first started work. He was also not a fan of the liberatory ideas Abdurrahman advocated, and which the students had begun to echo. Yet, while he might not have paid them much attention, he did not entirely ignore them. In light of his long managerial experience and expertise in dealing with different kinds of people, he just kept a wary eye on things without directly intervening, adopting a policy of containment rather than one of confrontation. He viewed revolutionary slogans and student zeal as no more than a summer cloud that would soon disperse without shedding a drop of rain or leaving any trace. What mattered was that those ideas should not disturb the peace and quiet of the school, that the school not be turned into a focal point for political criticism, and that the professors, students and staff remained true to the school's ethos, which was based on loyalty to the authorities and the absence of opposition.

* * *

One dusty morning on one of those burning hot May days, Abdurrahman was late to work, which was unusual for him. A colleague informed him that the director was expecting him in his office. Abdurrahman wasn't in his usual good mood that day. All that night he had lain awake in bed, unable to sleep because of the sandstorm and the marked increase in temperature that had accompanied it. Having finally fallen asleep shortly before the dawn prayer, he was awoken by the burning sun. He got up, washed his face, and brushed the grit of the storm off his bald head. Then he raced off to work, even forgetting to dab his neck and behind his ears with a few drops of the cologne he always carried with him.

Abdurrahman headed to the director's office, which was only a few paces from his own. He knocked twice on the door, then opened it and entered. The director was seated, legs crossed, behind his splendid desk, facing his team and some of his close collaborators. Abdurrahman said hello to them, but not one of them replied. After a pause, the director responded lukewarmly and asked him to sit.

The director addressed those sitting in front of him, as if resuming a discussion after Abdurrahman's entrance: "We must not allow anarchy to infiltrate our venerable institution. And we must not let destructive ideas spread among our students, to whom we must teach knowledge, commitment and allegiance to the nation and its wise leadership. Some have come with outlandish ideas, alien to the values and customs of our society, and want to engage the students in worthless cultural and political discussion. We must not allow that." He concluded in a sharp tone: "Have you understood?"

None of those present spoke, content to nod their heads in agreement.

Abdurrahman raised a finger, and before the director, who wanted to end the meeting, gave him permission to speak, he said: "Mr Director, only a fool would be deceived by this charade. The person you refer to is me, and those sitting in front of you are just extras in this badly-produced show. They know nothing about culture or politics, being the good-for-nothing products of your school, from which not a single political fighter has graduated in its history. It has, however, produced hundreds of spies, informants and yes-men, and the only movements they know are keeping their eyes to the ground.

"Yes, Mr Director, I am proud to spread revolutionary and progressive ideas among young people. And I am proud to practise and advocate politics, and oppose military rule and all dictatorships.

"As for your venerable school, as you described it and which is nothing of the sort, it is no honour to be associated with it. In the past, it was called LENA, and despite all its bad points was indeed *lena*, ours. But now it's become yours, *LACOM*, as if it were the property of your family business." And with that, Abdurrahman stormed out, slamming the door behind him.

Thus, in that moment of anger, the stacks of stories

came to an end, along with Abdurrahman's job at the library.

The whole business might have seemed surreal, except for the fact that those who knew Abdurrahman and understood his life knew that for him, the lines between the real and the surreal were not fixed, but often blurred or crossed. He was a man who could be roused to anger for the simplest reasons, and who was prepared to sacrifice himself for any cause, especially if the situation conflicted with his beliefs.

We tried to convince him to withdraw his resignation, telling him he had acted rashly in quitting the job that guaranteed him a monthly salary at a time when the country was in dire economic straits.

Our remonstrations did not convince him to change his mind. Together we wondered what he could do, given that he did not know how to manage on his own. Then a friend suggested that his next venture be a shop for telephone services.

* * *

I also left Guinea and its capital, Conakry. I found my work at the embassy boring, and the ambassador was a problem, too. He was determined to get his hands on the embassy budget, a matter made worse by the fact that there were only a few months left until he retired. My mood was one of despair because I was unable to keep my promise to the *sherif*, who had offered me a ro-

mantic life in Labé with four tall and beautiful Fulani
wives as well as a herd of cattle sufficient to endow me
with the wealth, esteem and status of an uncrowned
king.

My relationship with the ambassador had not been
easy or smooth from the day I had taken the embassy's
only car to a poor neighbourhood on the edge of the
capital to meet the most renowned fortune teller in
Guinea. As it happened, that was the day the ambassador
had been due to present his credentials to the President
of Guinea, and he was forced to take a taxi to the
Presidential Palace: an outcome which the ambassador
never forgave me for and which equally I never regretted.

The reading of shells, horoscopes, palms and coffee
cups fascinated me, and I was always seeking ways to
discern what lay beyond the horizon, and to reveal what
my future had in store. My belief in fortune tellers was
not one hundred percent as it often conflicted with
doubts arising from my religious culture. I knew for sure
that fortune tellers, even one as skilled and accurate as
Nostradamus, did not know the unseen world, and the
game of discovery became more like a hobby than a belief that was unshakeable and not hedged with doubts.

I had heard prophecies about my own life from many
mouths. Most, if not all, the "fortune tellers" had foreseen
wealth, status, prison and pleasure. They had seen both
easy paths and thorny dirt tracks strewn with obstacles.

Mariam specialised, she claimed, in communicating

with the dead and relaying news of their miserable or happy fates in the other world. To me she seemed convincing and the best of the cowrie shell diviners. She came out with a whole lot of things at once, but her language was clouded in ambiguity. Many of her prophecies came true, although sometimes in line with our proverb: Say much and something will be right.

From behind blond hair extensions, the Conakry fortune teller told me amazing things via a Guinean translator, who spoke the Arabic he had learned in Mauritania. Her voice turned hoarse, as if it were a cry emanating from unseen worlds: "You will return to buy what you fail to find and sell what you do not own."

This vague and ambiguous formula puzzled me, and I spent long nights seeking its key. I turned its associations and meanings over in my mind, but neither heart nor mind found rest. None of the interpretations seemed to relate to me, so I began to doubt her words, which seemed to have missed their target.

My endeavour to understand the fortune teller's riddle continued for a long time until the day Abdurrahman opened his 'call shop' – selling talk, as he described it. I became his partner and every day we planned how to make things work, and I gradually grew confident that the hidden meaning of the fortune teller's words was becoming clear.

* * *

I was on the move for many years and only ever spent a few days at a time in Nouakchott at best. So I never had enough time to explore the city and witness what they termed its enormous development. I wanted to believe the stories adorned with glossy pictures, but only felt disappointment.

My morning tour of Nouakchott revealed that three decades' worth of military rule had not brought dazzling results. The streets were full of potholes, stray buildings blocked the ends of streets, swarms of mosquitoes spread malaria, and hunger showed its talons in the faces of women and children.

The urban development seemed chaotic. Buildings sprouted haphazardly like mushrooms, and the sight of our capital shocked me. A decade earlier, I had witnessed its birth and early growth, and back then it had been simply a small town, but clean and organised, and had promised to be better in the future, even if the task were to prove difficult.

Many Mauritanians say that the French did not bequeath them a civilised capital. But how long did the French stay in Nouakchott? No more than twenty years. Yet instead of civilising the peoples of the Sahara that they colonised, they themselves became Bedouin, drinking tea, riding camels, and falling in love with fat women.

Before setting to work on the commercial venture with Abdurrahman, I had to go back to Nabaa for a time, away from the troubles afflicting the inhabitants of Nouakchott, which someone summed up as having all the bad points of a city with none of the benefits.

Nabaa remained a source of inspiration, even though that small village was growing into a town and also suffering from problems of roadbuilding and provision of services. That said, any disputes that arose were soon easily resolved with a kind word and courteous behaviour.

Thus I came to Nabaa to finish getting to know the many personalities Abdurrahman had told me about during our time abroad in Kuwait and Qatar. The character of Rajab the teacher, author of fine poetry and lover of more than one woman, fascinated me. At breakfast one morning I asked after him.

It wasn't hard to find him. There he was, walking down the main street, carrying his things on his head to keep off the sun, and followed by children reciting the Qur'an.

That day, however, I was unable to sit with him because he was in a bad mood. He had heard that a metalled road had been built across the encampments of Ghaylan (the eighth-century poet Dhu al-Rumma) in the Arabian Peninsula, and that Cadillacs had taken the place of the wild aurochs that grazed in the encampment of the poet's beloved, Mai. Rajab wept copiously in grief at the changes to the homeland of pre-Islamic poetry.

He had heard all about it from a son of Nabaa who had worked a long time in Saudi Arabia and who had also told him a piece of information he was hearing for the first time, namely that the town of Baalbek in Lebanon still existed. Now, Rajab would explain to his students when they reached the verse in Amr ibn Kalthoum's famous pre-Islamic poem, "How many goblets have I drunk in Baalbek, and others in Damascus and Qasirin", that Baalbek had been destroyed because its daughters were drunkards who spent night and day in the company of passing poets and those seeking the pleasures of the flesh.

I wandered around the landmarks of Nabaa after long absence. Fortunately, the first shop was as it had been, a cement and mud building with small, always-open doors and windows. Next to this old building, which stubbornly resisted the desert winds, stood a wall shaded by a mighty acacia tree.

With its usual spontaneity, the Society of Those Qualified to Bind and Unbind still met under that tree. No topics for discussion were agreed upon in advance and there was no agenda. Everything was conducted calmly and collectedly, and the meeting smoothly transitioned from a tea-drinking session into a session of binding and unbinding in which daily developments were discussed, and decisions quickly taken and immediately put into effect.

The Society almost invariably agreed when it came to worldly affairs, but when it came to religion, things were more complicated and discussions might be lengthy and heated, as if the rule had become disagreement and the exception consensus. The disputed topic would remain a bone of contention for a period that might often be prolonged.

For more than twenty years, since before my move to Madrid, when I was learning *hizb*s of the Qur'an from al-Majdhoub, a dispute had been raging between two camps at the mosque over the proper time for the dawn and sunset prayers. One side expedited and the other side delayed. The people of delay accused the people of expedition of praying before the correct time, while the people of expedition accused the other camp of praying after the due time. I found the dispute still intense, with each side mobilising whatever evidence it could muster in support of its position. I tried to make them see that the argument was one appropriate to the days of the Bedouin Arabs, and no longer justified in the age of modernity given the existence of clocks and watches. Nonetheless, neither side would listen to what I was saying or give it any credence.

The dispute over prayer times was not the only one engaging Nabaa. Religious disputes came floating to the surface with every new development affecting any vital aspect of life. For example, there was a quarrel over the loudspeaker. Was it permissible to use one for the call to prayer, or was it the mouthpiece of the Devil, Shaitan? Similarly with the compass. Was it permissible to rely on one to determine the direction for prayer, or should one be content with using the stars? Was the testimony of one radio sufficient to prove the sighting of the crescent moon, or were two radios required as some ruled?

The most recent of these disputes concerned the desire

of some young people to include an open-sided, covered area as part of the latest mosque expansion. The roots of the argument went back to the time when the village was founded. Back then, some wanted to build a mosque using cement and create an open area for Friday prayer, roofed with corrugated metal sheets to replace the existing trellis. However, some of the sheikhs were vehemently opposed to the idea, claiming that the trellis was endowed with *baraka* because the village's righteous ancestors had prayed there, not in a building made of cement and corrugated metal. The solution reached at that time kept the trellis where it was, with the mosque being constructed alongside. That solution, however, did not close the matter, but entrenched the dispute. The worshippers split into two groups: one that prayed under the trellis on the basis that that was the old mosque, and the other that prayed inside the new mosque. Those who prayed under the trellis were mostly the older generation, including my sheikh al-Majdhoub, while those who prayed inside the mosque were mostly the younger generations, who had travelled beyond the village, seen other towns and cities, read modern books, perused newspapers published in foreign countries, listened to the BBC, the Voice of America and Radio France International, and become familiar with modern lifestyles on the pilgrimage to Mecca, or on visits to Fes in Morocco, or while trading in Senegal. This dispute might have turned into a full-blown schism were it not for the spirit of affection and *baraka* that flowed in

Nabaa's waters, which everyone drank and which led both sides to an unspoken agreement whereby the obligatory prayers were performed inside the mosque, while each camp was free to perform the supererogatory prayers as they saw fit. As for non-obligatory prayers, the *dhikr* circles, praise sessions and Ramadan *taraweeh* prayers, they were performed under the trellis!

The trip gave me a chance to get to know Hussein the poet. Initially, I did not make his acquaintance in person, but by means of a poem that ripped through the village youth like fire through straw without anyone noticing. The poem's author was unknown, but its popularity and speed of transmission were mainly down to the sensitivity of its subject matter, namely that dark-skinned women were better than fair-skinned women. The poem went as follows:

By the pool in the depths of the glade
    a dark-eyed virgin delighted my heart.
Black, when we met she showed off her charms
    then concealed them as she pleased and seduced me.
Out of love for her, love of blacks haunted me
    everything black became of interest to me.
Appealing to the eye as she approached
    in the squares and in retreat hips swaying.
She seemed at twenty years old resplendent
    the day we met when she greeted me.
She seduced me; desire and my seventy years killing me
    the rest of my life promising plain old age.

> She had no respect for my white hair nor compassion
>   for my weakness and incapacity.
> Thus in the depths of the glade, girls of twenty
>   were there with men of eighty.
> I still conceal and reveal my love for her
>   my heart's desire between hidden and displayed.
> Today, I ask about her after she stamped my world
>   with desire. But will she preserve my faith?

Nobody knew exactly who had written the poem, which became more of a social issue than a literary one, and engaged everyone, young and old, men and women. Young men were fans of the poem, while it enraged their elders, who considered it outrageous. As for the women, it inflamed their jealousy, and their anger almost became mass hysteria. All the village's poets – no small number – were guilty until proven innocent, and for many of them married life became hell. Nine women started divorce proceedings with the local judge in which they accused their husbands of having composed the poem. All the judge could do was investigate and hear the cases, so he summoned the husbands, one by one, and confronted them with the accusation. Each swore the most solemn oath that he was as innocent of the poem as the wolf was of Joseph's blood.

"Investigations" undertaken by some to find the poem's author were inconclusive and rumours were rampant. Fingers were even pointed at the Toilers' Movement, which called, among other things, for mixed marriages between "whites" and "blacks" to end racism and strengthen the national fabric.

To make matters worse, Rajab the teacher got involved and promoted the poem widely. He would recite it in an amusing and ironic way when he visited gatherings of women. He might even make one of them believe her husband was the author, to make her mad with him. Then she would stomp out of the gathering in a reckless fury. Indeed, Rajab went further than that. He dared to write the poem down on the children's slates, upon which they studied the Qur'an, and instructed them to learn it by heart. He explained the meanings of the difficult words and tested them on the grammar and syntax, encouraging them in the endeavour by taking them early in the morning to the milking of his spoiled cows and letting them sip the froth on the fresh milk.

Hussein the poet was the last port of call for the ship of accusations regarding the authorship of the poem. This time, however, the charge was not laid by a woman motivated by jealousy or some ordinary fellow. No, it was Sheikh Ahmed, one of Nabaa's highly esieemed worthies, to whom God had granted an ample share of knowledge and flesh. He always wore a black robe and a green turban. A long string of prayer beads hung down from his neck, which he never took off, not even when he went to sleep. The one hundred beads ranged in colour from crimson red to bright yellow and nestled among the amulets covering his chest to form a polychromatic abstract painting that alluded to the medals and ribbons of a First World War hero.

Ahmed was highly respected because of his amazing ability to memorise things. He was reputed to have memorised everything he had ever read or heard, and once he'd memorised something, he never forgot it. As a result, he served as the village's memory and its living archive. The old men relied on him to recount the history of the tribe and recall its glories and boasts. The children also loved him. They crowded around him, tugging at the hem of his robe whenever they bumped into him in the street. He would hand out the sweets that filled his pockets and the children's faces would light up in delight. For me, Sheikh Ahmed was the local version of Papa Noel, whom I watched roaming the streets of Madrid at the New Year's holiday.

In addition to all those virtues, Sheikh Ahmed was renowned for dealing in the "secrets of the letters", the magic that gave him the power to harness the jinn, bend the laws of nature, and read the unseen and people's secrets.

How did Sheikh Ahmed uncover the secret of the poem's author? Did one of the jinn tell him? He didn't say so explicitly, but some of those who asked him the question inferred it from his ambiguous answers, which bore more than one meaning and interpretation. Did he in fact recognise Hussein the poet's style or "voice", as some said, given his long experience and wide knowledge of Hussein's poetry? No one knew, and Sheikh

Ahmed did not reveal the sources of his information, although some reckoned the latter possibility was more likely, because if it had been the jinn who told him, he would have said so outright for the record, as had happened on previous occasions when he had relied on information derived from the jinn to silence his opponents!

Hussein the poet getting the blame for writing the poem had a positive effect on the social atmosphere in Nabaa. It meant that many other men were acquitted of the heinous charge that had almost ended their marriages, and that lowered the temperature of jealousy and tension among the women to customary levels. Family life resumed its usual affectionate course.

Hussein the poet did not comment on the accusation and did not give it much thought. He did not confess, but at the same time he did not plead his innocence, content to say that intention was louder than words, which some took as an implicit confession.

I met him in the midst of a group of men under the shade of a trellis not far from the shop premises where the Society of Those Qualified to Bind and Unbind held their meetings. They introduced us, as I had not met him before. He was sitting silently on a palm fibre mat, smoking a pipe made from a sheep's bone and exhaling the smoke upwards out of politeness to those present. It seemed that the discussion over the poem ascribed to him, which I had not been present for, was dying down. In fact, it had been no ordinary discussion but more of a trial. All eyes were on Hussein, awaiting his response.

It came soon enough. "If it was not me who wrote the poem, there is no doubt that its author spoke in my voice and uttered what I feel. As everybody here knows, I prefer one dark woman to a thousand of the tribe's white women. Do you not know that true love has no colour, gentlemen?"

Then he began reciting verses from the poem, pointing out their finer points. His commentary elicited the approval of some of those present who had been bold enough to praise the poem, its clever arrangement and honest lyricism. Others simply smiled, while some left the meeting in protest at the insinuations against fair-skinned women and the preference for black women. I was with the first group and took the unenviable position of defending the poem, praising its artistic features despite my total ignorance of the criteria of criticism and my scanty stock of poetry. I remember describing the poet as a genius, the Nelson Mandela of Arabic poetry, fighting against racial discrimination. I even asked for the poem to be written out in gold and hung on the door of the shop, as well as being taught to children, as Sheikh Rajab was doing.

The audience were stunned at the force and daring of my intervention. I felt a sense of pride that somebody else shared my idea of rebelling against tribal values, and that Hussein the poet approved of what I had said, even though, as he told me later, he was unable to decipher the riddle of some of the strange words coming out of my mouth that he was hearing for the first time.

I went up to him and hailed him: "God reward you, Hussein. You said what I and many others think."

He gave a wry smile and said: "Things in our society are upside down. In most of the world, women are under the thumb of men and fight for their liberation. But in our society, men are under the thumb of women and happy about it. In fact, all our men are the victims of their wives, but they play the role of the one wielding the knife while the woman plays the role of the sacrificial lamb. Men in our society have to free themselves from the sway and tyranny of women!"

Hussein was never married, not even for one night, as Rajab the teacher had been. He kept away from women, but was close to them at the same time, or as he would say, he kept away in order to get closer. He remained hesitant, but free in his desires, open to dark colours and the hidden fruits of the body. He preferred to be an eternal bachelor, spending months of the year on the Shamama Plains in southern Mauritania where tribal authority did not hold sway, moving from locale to locale, falling in love with dark-skinned women, be they as sturdy as zebras or as delicate as gazelles.

I became warm friends with Hussein despite the difference in age between us. I found he possessed an elegance of speech, a sense of humour and a memory that held thousands of poems.

Hussein the poet told me about the plains and hills in the Mauritanian south, about dark-skinned women, about planting, sowing and life on the banks of rivers, and the pleasure of life far removed from the control of the tribe. In his words I sensed the passion of vagabond poets for rebellion and the linguistic refinement of the poets of Al-Andalus.

Over one long night, I told him about the European cities I had visited and my experiences with the women I had got to know in those cities, some of whom I had fallen in love with. Yet what he was most interested in was the highlands of the Fouta Djallon in Guinea, our cousin who still lived like an uncrowned king in Labé, and his wives, servants, followers and Sufi *zawiya*. Hussein was sorry he could not join him, after so many trains on the rusty railway of life had already passed.

During our evenings, which extended until dawn, and during my long, almost uninterrupted conversations with him, I often felt he was leading me towards moments of deep doubt over the worth and meaning of life. I felt he had seamlessly drawn me towards the verdant world to the south, a place of music and poetry, sowing and reaping.

I became a regular at Hussein's gatherings, which brought together poets and writers from across the community and went on until very late at night. The poets would compete to compose odes and verses in classical Arabic and the vernacular, and to recall poems and stories from the glory days of the Arabs.

I didn't really participate in the gatherings, content just to listen as my pleasure in them caused time to vanish and long nights to melt into nothingness like a block of ice on a sunny day.

* * *

After two weeks in which I nourished my weary spirits, the time came to return to Nouakchott. I had, as they say today, recharged my batteries. I enjoyed the poetry sessions and met with men I had missed since childhood, having left Nabaa thirty years before. Previously, I had come on fleeting visits of only a few hours, sufficient time to see family. Immersing myself in the world of Nabaa and its stories, and getting close to its characters, was not something I had ever thought of doing. In fact, if it hadn't been for Abdurrahman, that treasure trove would have remained under lock and key, out of reach, its pearls sealed inside their shells.

I was saddened by the fate of al-Majdhoub, who had gone away shortly before my arrival on a journey from which he was never to return. He would set off on a journey whenever some hidden impulse urged him, and the absence of any means of transport was no obstacle. They were all the same to him, so he did not wait around for a car, a camel or an ass. The summer heat or winter cold was no impediment. He would take to the road and walk alone, accompanied by a container of water for drinking and abluting, and a few handfuls of peanuts, plus whatever fate had in store for him.

Before he set off, he said goodbye to the folk of Nabaa,

one by one. To his friends at the mosque, after dancing for hours and reciting poems of panegyric, love and glorification of the self and the tribe, he said he was going somewhere they would never see him.

Some thought that was a hint of what was to come in the following days. Others blocked their ears, as they did when the man had a manic turn, but no one took al-Majdhoub's words seriously.

A week passed after his departure and there was no news. Then a salt caravan found him lying on the path as if he'd been asleep forever. He had departed this life, his hand clutching his *sibha* beads. His metal water container had melted in the sun, and his desiccated body was nearly becoming food for the circling vultures. The wind, whose fury had not abated since his death, also whipped around him, throwing up dust to cover him. It was said at the time that he had been going to visit his mother's grave, but Death took him when he was halfway there.

Abdurrahman, who was stunned by the news, said: "That manic man was created for a bygone age."

The sheikhs of the community eulogised him, then went their separate ways. His memory lingered briefly like bounteous white clouds that the wind soon disperses far beyond the limits of eye and ear. The sheikhs forgot him and waited for another manic man to appear, as always in beloved Nabaa.

* * *

Abdurrahman held a modest opening party for his new base, offering telephone and fax services. His close friends and some investors attended, me among them. The premises were at the intersection of two main roads, close to a big hotel that had recently opened its doors. From a commercial perspective, the location was excellent, and even according to the most pessimistic estimates Abdurrahman was set to make a healthy profit. That would allow him to settle some of the debts he had racked up while working at the library, as well as helping him meet many of the commitments he had taken on, and perhaps even save something for the future.

Abdurrahman welcomed his first customer exuberantly. He offered him a glass of hot tea with mint and a few peanuts and biscuits, and inquired about his family, job and education. When the customer had finished his call, which lasted almost an hour, he took a banknote out of his pocket to pay, but Abdurrahman said he had decided in advance that the first call would be free. He had not, however, expected the call to be so long. Even so he would not go back on his decision, even if all the world's telephone companies went bankrupt as a result. Abdurrahman said goodbye to the customer, who left laughing.

The words of the fortune teller concerning the sale of what I did not own were still on my mind. If that didn't mean talk, I wondered, what could it be?

I went every morning to the phone centre to meet

Abdurrahman, and our friendship grew closer day by day. The different kinds of customers gradually became clear. There was passing trade, especially guests at the nearby hotel, but there were also regulars who used the centre's services in a city that was devoid of them.

A young journalist from Senegal made the centre his bureau. Still taking his first steps in the media field, he came in every evening, gabbed incessantly, and built up a substantial tab each month. He always settled late because he had to wait for payment from the media organisations he worked for. Instead of paying what he owed, he gave a smirk and offered bizarre excuses that revealed the breadth of his imagination.

Abdurrahman's patience with the journalist often ran out, especially when the national postal service sent the monthly phone bill. Then the swindler journalist would resort to diverting Abdurrahman's attention towards other worlds as far removed from concern about his bill as possible. He would tell him so many stories – about the hermetic world of the city's margins, incidents that had happened in the dark labyrinths of police cells, details of ridiculous courtroom proceedings, unbelievable love stories of the rich and famous – all the product of his unruly imagination. In this way, the trickster always found a way to satisfy the man in charge. He sold him stories in exchange for phone calls and created tales and excuses that delighted him, all accompanied with a dazzling smile, so that in the end, Abdurrahman gave him more time to pay.

There was also Li the Chinaman. His being a regular customer touched a soft spot with Abdurrahman and reawakened his dormant left-wing tendencies, evoking Mao's cultural revolution and the Toilers' Movement. The new Chinaman, like his government, competed with capitalists on their own terms, but without dropping the socialist façade.

In the knowledge that when Nouakchott slept, Shanghai was awake, Abdurrahman sometimes dozed off. The Chinese city in the Far East would be bustling as Nouakchott in the West readied itself for sleep, its streets deserted. Then the eyes of the staff at the call shop would grow heavy, but they remained on alert for Li, a regular customer of the night, which made him different to the others.

Abdurrahman smiled as he followed the footsteps of the Chinaman, who spoke broken French in an accent that made it hard to make out the words. That didn't matter provided Li remained alone with the telephone receiver, chatting for an hour or more. Then he took out a bundle of blue banknotes in the national currency and paid the exact amount of his bill, before disappearing into the dark.

What with the Chinaman and the customers from the hotel next door, every day at the centre was pretty much the same. Abdurrahman would be happy at times, reassured that his decision to try capitalist methods had been correct, having exhausted himself talking about the virtues of socialism. In this way, days at the centre ticked over until the arrival of an elegant, sweet-talking Jordanian man, Nabil, who made calls with no regard for the cost in half a dozen languages and to a score of countries, East and West.

Nabil would arrive with a young man, who it later transpired was his son. These two Jordanians made the call shop in Nouakchott their personal office. Abdurrahman liked having them around and opened his heart to them. They reminded him of the time he had spent in the Arab East, especially when they offered him the opportunity of a lifetime to get rich quick, by means of an idea no one had thought of before.

The two Jordanians had the revolutionary idea of turning African scrap metal into gold. They explained their plan to him as follows: "Scrap vehicles, bits of railway track, washing machines, rebars, wire, nails, broken parts. Anything made of iron or metal you can think of that is discarded as junk can be collected and shipped to the markets of East Asia, where factory machines work round the clock opening their maws to ingest every substance on earth. It's a goldmine, Abdurrahman. Just say the word, join hands with us, and we can turn iron into gold."

Sitting next to them, I thought it sounded like a brilliant idea. We spent hours calculating and recalculating the profits to be made from selling African scrap metal to two Jordanians, who were willing, as they said, to pay upfront. I opened my bag and took out my address and telephone book, which was full after years spent roaming the world. My expertise as an accountant would also come in useful. I remembered what I had said to Abdurrahman when we were sitting drinking green tea at the call shop: "This is our last chance to join the rich man's club. The two Jordanians have got the cash, the scrap iron is in Africa, and us two, we'll just be agents. We won't lose anything and we'll gain a lot."

"We'll be agents, then. What a lousy profession!" said Abdurrahman, but he was smiling gently and did not object. What I had said struck a chord with him and he seemed confident that the moment of truth had come. I realised at the time, as I tempted him to throw himself into a venture whose risks were unknown, that we could both sense the tantalising proximity of wealth, like any dreaming alchemist.

I had to sell everything I owned to be able to travel in search of the stuff the Jordanians were after. I would go back to Conakry, visit Dakar and Lomé, make the rounds of piles of rusting junk, and get to know scrap merchants. I would also cast an eye over ports chock-a-block with old cars that had never cleared customs. Abdurrahman would come with me on the journey in search of the goods, whose promise of profits had made him forget about the call shop. He left it under the supervision of one of his relatives on the grounds that he was busy with something more worthwhile, important, and closer to the world of finance and business.

The Jordanians asked Abdurrahman to let them have a room in the centre to use as an office for their activities, given the availability of telephones and fax machines. This was to be counted as part of Abdurrahman's contribution to the project's costs. Of course, Abdurrahman agreed in good faith, without any thought of the bill at the end of the month.

One morning, a tall, thin, dark-skinned woman joined the Jordanian team. She had a childish face and a permanent half-smile on her lips. When Nabil introduced her to us as their organisation's PR person, Abdurrahman gave me a meaningful look, but I ignored it and turned to examine the girl's face, which reminded me of something as yet unknown but already lodged deep in my heart.

The girl, whose name was Silva, came from a Caribbean island, one formerly part of the empire on which the sun never set, but her face did not reflect the magic I had seen in Teresa, despite her dark complexion.

For Abdurrahman the girl did not bode well. He saw that she spoke to her family in the West Indies at length without consideration for the bill that would join others like it in the iron office safe.

Over time, as these new consumerist habits grew worse, Abdurrahman stopped thinking about management. He no longer asked about sales, or the debts that used to keep him awake at night. His attention was devoted to the scrap metal venture and the large profits he was expecting. In contrast, paying the phone bill became difficult without sufficient liquidity.

We were approaching the end of another experience

on the turbulent path of our lives. We were standing at the edge of a volcano's crater, the seductive colours of the abyss that could melt gold drawing us ever nearer, while the thick clouds of vapour stopped us seeing where our feet were.

It did not take long to discover that all of us, but especially Abdurrahman, had been duped big time. The two Jordanians and their black Girl Friday disappeared one day without trace, leaving behind a pile of unpaid bills. Fortunately or not, we were not the only ones to fall victim to the gang. The day after their disappearance, a large crowd of their victims gathered in front of the call shop seeking information. There was the landlord who'd rented them an apartment for seven months without them having paid any rent. The boss of a car rental place was looking for his luxury Mercedes, which had vanished with them. The owner of the restaurant where they ate every day. And so on. Abdurrahman gave a relaxed smile and, as if giving a sermon to his followers, said: "Your losses could have been much worse. This is the fate of those who engage in business and bow to rapacious capitalism."

I remembered my holy fool sheikh, who now appeared before me in the guise of Abdurrahman, reinstating his deep-rooted leftist culture. He wiped the dust off his face with the hem of his black robe, checking at the same time that the perfume he had sprayed onto it had not lost its effect. Then he continued addressing the crowd of creditors and curious bystanders: "I too have lost everything because I submitted to the temptations of greed. But money isn't everything. If you look for it again, you will find it."

Most of them became angry, and nearly pushed him into one of his occasional nervous outbursts, but he kept calm as he bade a final farewell to business.

Once Abdurrahman had finished speaking and advising the victims of the gang, I was certain there was no point in getting further into debt by having to pay what the office owed at the end of the month. The spectre of bankruptcy, which had always hovered over the office, had become a fact. Closure was inevitable, but even so, Abdurrahman, with his excessive kindness, failed to comprehend that it was never going to be possible to turn Africa's scrap metal – however great the quantity – into riches and glory.

After the call shop was declared bankrupt, the police sealed it the with red wax. Abdurrahman insisted on turning its closure into the occasion for a party, during which he gave a rousing speech to two members of staff and a few old customers. He warned them of the treachery of worldly affairs and exhorted them to be patient and not to surrender to savage capitalism.

His speech was a melange of al-Ma'arrian asceticism, Confucian wisdom and Guevarian leftism, spiced with proverbial lore, common sense and some flirtatious lines from his teacher Rajab.

Wavering between tears and laughter, I watched what might be considered his valedictory address. It all reminded me of an incident in which Abdurrahman had set fire to a bundle of banknotes during an argument with a customer over the tariff for a phone call.

Abdurrahman attached no significance to money. In fact, he said he wasn't seeking money but freedom. His aim in life, he frequently said, was not to be rich but to be poor and free. He often repeated in our hearing: "O Lord, O Lord, by the Sura of the Sand Dunes, be generous and give us barely enough."

War Dance at Kanz al-Asrar[*]

In the latest wave of drought, Nouakchott was going through the worst of times. The rains had stopped falling and clouds of dust had formed a black cloak over the city. Powerful sandstorms blasted the capital and reduced visibility on the roads, causing fatal accidents. The authorities frequently had to close the airport to international flights. An open crescent of sand dunes advancing from the Sahara was besieging the city from the east and the north in a pincer movement, and cutting it off from the towns of the interior.

To the west, the barrier of sand that divided the capital from the ocean waves had been eroded as a result of unplanned urban development, which had boomed under the anarchy of military rule. This led international experts to warn that the capital, which was located below sea level, risked inundation unless steps were taken before it was too late. The warning didn't come only from environmentalists and oceanographers. One of the well-

---

[*] Hoard of Secrets

known holy men of the city prophesised its imminent destruction. He said that when he was awake, and not dreaming, he had seen it transformed into desolate ruins haunted by screeching owls and inhabited by packs of wolves while the wind howled through it. An even gloomier prediction was made in a novel by one of the country's writers, who said the city would become a dumping ground for nuclear waste from the Eastern Mediterranean.

The warnings of experts, the sheikh's vision, the writer's novel, and the rumours over the rising sea level, all created a tense atmosphere of fear and insecurity in the capital. Disaster nearly struck one morning when the waves breached the sand barrier and engulfed large areas of dry land just five kilometres south of the city. This set off a wave of panic among the inhabitants, some of whom decided to quit the city and head for towns and villages in the interior, which were far from the shore and so safer.

Abdurrahman also woke me up early one morning and, almost choking in the midst of a severe bout of asthma brought on by the particles carried in a dust storm, said: "We have to get out of this city that oppresses its people. I heard a report on the BBC this morning about the threats to coastal cities as a result of global warming. You don't know, but Nouakchott is one of the cities at greatest risk. Imagine one of the dormant undersea volcanoes in the Atlantic erupts. It will cause a ferocious tsunami that might swallow up the city and everything and everyone in it. Where can we find safety? Where to run?"

On the same subject, I said: "Did you know that I visited our sheikh last night? He came to visit Nouakchott, which is unlike him, and told me his vision, straight from his mouth to my ears. A terrifying dream. I drank tea with him and we talked about many things. It was strange, but he opened his heart to me and revealed some very personal things. This sheikh only talks about personal matters with those he trusts, as you know."

Abdurrahman frowned, so I added: "We were drinking green tea together and the sheikh was relaxed and expansive, talking about his vision, which everyone's talking about. He told me stories of the saints' and holy men's wonders and miracles. Things never before seen or heard or felt in the human heart. I listened to him reverently as though a bird were perched on my head. Suddenly, he turned to me and began telling me things about my life. As if he were reading from an open book. Yes, he told me about some of my personal secrets, ones I have kept buried deep down. Yes, my personal secrets, highly personal. Do you remember that young British woman who was with the Jordanian businessman?"

"You mean Silva?"

"Yes, Silva, that's her. Well, I used to have a date with her every evening after her friend went out to make his calls from your office. We might go to the beach, far from sight, and have some fun."

Abdurrahman broke in angrily: "And when you came

back from the beach, Silva would pick up the phone and call her family. She's responsible for the bureau going bust, and you were in fact her partner in that. I swear, I was certain a catastrophe was going to befall us when I first saw you giving her the eye."

I tried to steer the conversation away a little and resumed where I had left off earlier.

"The sheikh is a righteous man and his vision is as clear as day. It's said that he once sent word to the President when he was in a cabinet meeting to warn him of an imminent attack by the Polisario Front against the capital, Nouakchott. The President had barely managed to end the meeting when a barrage of bazooka fire hit the Presidential Palace. By the grace of God, everyone escaped the attack. Miraculous. When the President asked where the warning had come from, the sheikh pointed to his veil!"

Can you believe it, a veil talks and reveals secrets and military plans? Of course, the answer is no, but it was a true story.

* * *

Early in the morning we took a car to the village of Kanz al-Asrar, a small place by one of the tributaries of the Senegal River. To begin with, we crossed a dangerous area of elevated sands, leaving behind a sandstorm. Then we descended gently to the southwest, as if we were on the path that would liberate us from the folly of the age and the burden of guilt. And suddenly we were overlooking the green valley, which was only bounded by the distant river. The spectacle took our breath away, and at first we could not believe our tired eyes were seeing a chain of oases reaching as far as the horizon. This made the flat expanse of the western Saharan uplands a safe place, and turned the vast stretch into a lush paradise.

Abdurrahman and I spent ten hours in a Land Rover crossing from the desert expanses to the edge of the unspoiled region, which stretched out without limit. The village of Kanz al-Asrar was on the Shamama Plains, where former slaves lived in small villages on the edgse of the fertile plain irrigated by the flood of the Senegal River. These numerous villages were a refuge for all those who wanted to relax and listen to music in a place alive with song and the intoxication of freedom.

Having escaped their masters, slaves settled in these small villages. Kanz al-Asrar, however, seemed a land in limbo, along with its inhabitants. They dwelled there, caught between the freedom bubbling in the surrounding villages and the stringent regime imposed by the sheikh on his followers. They had joined him in this place free of sadness and pain, an isolated vestige of the Garden of Eden. The white houses of the village cast their shadows over a watercourse that wrapped around it on three sides and formed the source of the inhabitants' livelihood. They planted grain, caught small river fish and raised the finest cattle.

The moment we arrived at the northern entrance to Kanz al-Asrar, Hussein the poet was returning from his morning rounds. He was wont to walk for a while along the watercourse, before taking his clothes off and bathing in the river, washing off the dirt, as he was accustomed to describing that intimate moment.

When we met the poet, he was clearheaded and in a fine mood. He was a world away from malicious gossips and spent his time between the assemblies of the sheikh, with their audiences of listeners, where beautiful poems would be chosen and sung by one of the sheikh's wives or daughters, and his walks on the grassy paths between the fields, or just sitting contemplating creation in the form of virgin nature.

He gave us a picture of life in Kanz and told us a few of the rules that had to be followed: "Don't smoke. Cigarettes are forbidden as well as any kind of tobacco. If you want to smoke, do it in secret and far off. The sheikh has an incredible sense of smell, and in any case his eyes are legion, everywhere around the village."

I had no desire to smoke, having won my battle with it years ago. My last cigarette, or rather my last cigar, was a present from the Cuban ambassador in Madrid. I smoked it with pleasure as we talked in the garden of his residence on an occasion marking the Cuban revolution, which I was keen on celebrating for one reason: watching the legs of the Cuban girls who came to the Embassy for fear that they would be branded agents of the CIA and blacklisted if they did not turn up.

We went to the sheikh's assembly and found him at the centre of a circle of his disciples in an atmosphere of reverent tranquillity. Everyone was listening attentively to the seventy-year-old man speaking about the miracles of the righteous, and the stations and trances of the Sufis. From time to time, a female voice singing beautiful poetry interrupted the sheikh. We could not tell exactly where the voice was coming from, because the women were somewhere behind him and could not be seen.

The voice sang beautifully and the sheikh was captivated. Along with his students he was drawn towards love of the divine and demanded more of the melody, which was unaccompanied by any instrument. When it reached a nirvana-like climax, he called on his disciple Zaydan to sing.

Zaydan knew all the odes and melodies that delighted the sheikh, but he did not venture to transport him too much, because that might risk the sheikh's life. The last time he had sung al-Buseiri's poem rhyming in *meem*, the sheikh had spent two days unconscious in bed, unable to control his limbs.

Hussein ushered in the renowned Ispinniyat band, a group of six men, six women and a *tidinet* player. He did not ask permission from the sheikh – Hussein was the only individual who could act without referring to him. The sheikh, however, respected the decision of a poet like Hussein, who had abandoned all the tribe's villages to come and live with him in his remote one.

The band had come to Kanz al-Asrar, where the few

cement houses were strung out along one of the river's tributaries. The inhabitants laid carpets between the sheikh's house and the stream to allow the dancers to perform the war dance.

The melody of the *ardeen* player roused the sheikh from the siesta that he took assiduously since it helped him cope with long nights of prayer and worship. The female player strummed the strings with her fingertips, releasing silvery notes, flowing like a river. The sheikh smiled at the surge of ecstasy inside him and gave the signal to Hussein the poet to start the party.

A wide chair with armrests and covered with a rug was set down for the sheikh so he could follow the nimble dancers from that prominent position. Male dancers carried spears and wooden swords that symbolised battle, while female dancers moved between the two groups, encouraging each side to victory.

The women swayed quickly and gracefully, following each other's footsteps, their legs decorated with henna patterns and plant designs. Their feet, however, moved in a slow, steady rhythm that echoed the movements of their hands and arms, which rose and fell in an effort to grab hold of something. Yet the dancing fingers, also decorated with henna, were unable to find this something during their tireless search. The eyes of the onlookers shone, burning with an inner fire as they watched the dancing fingers challenge the space around them like flames reaching up to the sky. As rhythm and music grew riotously, capturing the souls of the women

dancers, the ranks of the men opposite them exploded
into motion. Perhaps they had been like the dead,
slaughtered by wounds of desire. Now they used their
wooden swords to smite an invisible enemy. The
women, bare-chested, enflamed the heat of the battle
where life encountered death. As the musicians reached
a crescendo, it was as if oil poured onto the fires of desire
and blood, and water poured onto the fire burning in
the heart. But still the fire of the male and female dancers
was inextinguishable, and refused a truce between life
and death.

Laughing like a happy child, the sheikh said: "The
women are inciting war!" Everyone laughed and ululations reverberated forth. Abdurrahman and I sat there
watching the party up close, shifting our gaze between
the ecstatic sheikh and the poet who was improvising
verses in praise of the bounty of creation for the singers
to immediately repeat.

The melodies interwove, shifting from key to key; the
dancing bodies swayed to the sound of the instruments.
The poet looked overjoyed as he composed new lyrical
stanzas that flowed in a cascade from the wells of his
being, genre after genre: panegyric, love for dark-
skinned girls and, finally, praise for the sheikh and lyrics
about his miracles and elevated morals.

I observed the state of spiritual ecstasy possessing the
sheikh's faithful disciple, Zaydan. Since the beginning
of the party, he had been waiting for a sign from his
sheikh, because naturally he could not dance to this rich

music without his permission. Then came the moment when the sheikh gave his disciple Zaydan permission to dance. The musician was warming up a tune that the crowd knew would send Zaydan into orbit, and there was a tacit complicity for the rest of the band to play the tune, too.

Zaydan emerged from behind the audience wrapped in a cloak the sheikh had given him as a present, and wearing a veil, as was customary for great dancers. He began his steps to the ululation of the women and the clapping of the men. He raised his slender legs and gave a half-pirouette before squatting down, then leaping up. He continued dancing until he was foaming at the mouth in ecstasy. And then he passed out in the arms of the sheikh, who stroked his brow with a pale hand.

The sheikh stayed sitting quite still. He understood the spiritual state his disciple was in, so he left him to shiver and foam at the mouth and mumble incomprehensible words. He remained like that for about an hour, during which time the party did not stop. The music itself was a cure for Zaydan's condition, after he fell, slain on the battlefield of divine love as he entered the bottomless depths of spiritual ecstasy.

I found being in Kanz al-Asrar highly enjoyable, and Abdurrahman felt the same. Between the sheikh and Hussein the poet, a rare affection developed that allowed the party to go on until very late at night. Hussein re-cited poetry, played melodies and told many stories of the saints. The atmosphere took me back to my childhood in Nabaa and the assemblies of my grandfather, which were of a Sufi tenor, when my soul would soar away into the Kingdom.

Kanz's houses were few in number and it lacked a market, but fruits were brought from everywhere. This was a cause of happiness for Abdurrahman and stimulated his appetite for a different style of life, one unconnected to the material world, with no room for talk of money and luxury.

In his oneness with Kanz al-Asrar, Abdurrahman met poets, dancers, and *tidinet* players, but what truly delighted and entranced him was a woman he met one autumn evening. Her pale face still bore the traces of a faded beauty and her ample body indicated that in the past she had seen much meat and fat.

That Woman's Name is Mounira

She drew Abdurrahman's attention as she sat in a quiet corner of the party away from the crowd. He noticed that although she was following the action with great interest, she was the only woman who appeared to be a stranger and not completely integrated. With his singular ability to understand people, he sensed that this woman had an unusual story.

Her demeanour was calm and poised, so he approached cautiously and, just as Zaydan was about to start dancing again to his favourite melody, he asked her his usual question: "Where have you come from? Please tell me a little about yourself." An annoying question perhaps, but it came with a weak smile and a hard stare into space, which was sometimes rather sad and unfocused. Such was his way of coaxing people to talk about themselves, so he could hear about the paths in life ordinary people had taken and delve into the mysteries of their personalities.

One might expect those on the receiving end of the question to be annoyed, but surprisingly they would start talking, submitting to the irresistible power of their own story. Abdurrahman, as I always said, possessed the lubricant that opened up what people kept closed. Those he questioned soon instinctively grasped that the intention was not to annoy or pester them, but reflected a person who was open to knowledge, seeking an understanding of humanity's distinct cultures and lives.

In an even tone, Mounira said she suspected she knew more about him than he knew about her, especially the period of his childhood. She then asked him a surprising question: "Are you one of the sons of Nabaa?"

Abdurrahman laughed his resonant laugh and told her her suspicions were right on the mark. "Yes, I am indeed a son of Nabaa. But how did you know, my dear old lady?" As he spoke, he stole glances at her beautiful face, assuming she would not notice his boldness in staring at her beauty, which exceeded the desert night in its splendour.

Mounira brushed what looked like specks of dust off her face, raised from the ground by the energetic dancing. "If my memory does not betray me," she replied, "I can also take a guess at who you are. Aren't you one of the lads who accompanied Rajab the teacher when he used to visit our district, which was not far from Nabaa?"

Abdurrahman gave a cry of recognition. His memory had begun to reveal scenes in which the same woman appeared, but in the bloom of youth. He saw her inside her tent, which provided her with a veil of secrecy that concealed the amorous visits of Rajab the teacher. She

was, after all, already married, and feared the anger of
her jealous husband.

The utterly amazed Abdurrahman had not meant to
brush against Mounira's hennaed hand, but that's exactly
what happened. He raised his hand to his mouth to hide
an emerging smile, and while the hand was returning to
where it ought to be, it met Mounira's, which was ar-
ranging her clothing and brushing off the dust. When
the two hands touched, their eyes met in a moment that
had the impact of a bolt of lightning. "Such a moment
condenses life from birth to end," he thought to himself.

* * *

The night had drawn in and the dancers and the
crowd left the open space in front of the sheikh's house.
Abdurrahman and I accompanied the woman, whose
name, *Mounira* – "she who brings light" – lit up our
night-time path. We helped carry her things towards the
nearby village, where she lived as a widow with some
of her family.

When we arrived there, they brought us a mattress and
placed it next to the canvas tent where the family lived.
Then they brought green tea and cow's milk and we
launched into a long conversation under the watch of
the glimmering stars, stars so close one could almost
touch them.

For what remained of the night, Abdurrahman and
Mounira exchanged the details of a shared history. It was

exciting for me to hear it all, it was as if I were listening to the chapters of a wonderful novel whose details were inscribed on loving hearts.

Their conversation about Rajab the teacher went on and on, covering his amusing stories, his poetry, and his tricks, which no one escaped but all accepted with good grace.

Mounira had been Rajab the teacher's first love. He fell absolutely and totally in love with her and had eyes for no other woman. He took any chance he could to visit her, with or without any excuse. Like a poet of old from a vanished world, he would send her lines of poetry praising her beauty. It was a chaste love, as pure and sinless as water, just as Ghaylan or Qais ibn al-Mulawwah had loved. They were the poets closest to Rajab's heart, and he emulated them to the point of impersonation.

Mounira recalled her memories of Abdurrahman's teacher, while Abdurrahman seemed stupefied as he shook his head like a man possessed, before laughing hysterically. She took pains to explain every detail, unveiling stories in her own sweet resonant voice, as if embellishing the teacher's endless tales. From time to time, she took Abdurrahman's hand and they plunged together into captivating labyrinths.

I watched the absentminded glances across the space between them and listened to the conversation. They seemed to be acting out roles in a black-and-white Egyptian film that ends with the hero discovering that the girl he's talking to is none other than his sister, or neighbour at the very least, after time has separated them for many years.

We spent the night under the light of joyous gleaming stars floating in blackness. A shy half moon looked down from not far above revealing with its blueish rays the features of the few objects around us. Every so often, we heard the lowing of cows from nearby and the hissing of a large snake that lived alone in these flatlands but caused no harm. Sometimes the vast silence was broken by the croaking of frogs that swam in the many ponds.

In the morning we returned to Kanz al-Asrar. Time seemed like a river running its course, racing to its end, that we passed along every day without capturing its essence. Had we really been here a whole month without realising? Was the river flowing next to us or were we flowing next to it, helping us discover that our days were joy, dance and spiritual ecstasy, and our nights devoted to poetry, Sufi hymns and glasses of green tea effusing the scent of gum Arabic?

Zaydan, the sheikh's preferred messenger whom he entrusted with important tasks, came and asked us to attend the sheikh's assembly. We recognised his voice in the distance. A voice that soared above the patches of green infused with the all-encompassing daylight. To the layered rhythms of his deep voice, the words of his favourite song filled the ripening verdure as far as the horizon. Nobody would deny Zaydan the pleasure of rhapsodising about his imaginary beloved, whom he described as the most beautiful daughter of Eve, tall and plump like a block of soft marble the colour of milk and with a heart of honey, like most of Kanz's women.

Stifling his singing, which could be heard around after he left the sheikh's house, Zaydan said to us: "The sheikh invites you to his assembly." Then he smiled, showing his even white teeth. The tone of his voice hinted at something about the invitation being different from those we had received every day before.

At twilight, the awesome sheikh of Kanz welcomed us. He was seated on his red carpet, playing the beads of his *sibha* through his fingers. He murmured words of divine praise or prayer, which no one could make out. He shook our hands, then without preliminaries asked about the woman we had accompanied back to her family the night before.

The sheikh's question hinted at a detailed knowledge of events. He wished to signal that nothing was hidden from him.

Zaydan smiled and without waiting for the sheikh's permission to speak, said: "Sidi al-sheikh, your pupil among the jinn must have informed you."

The sheikh laughed but did not answer his disciple. It was a sign to us that his sources of information were not limited to human beings alone, but included the jinn, who provided him with accurate reports of events hidden from others.

Addressing us, the sheikh said: "You have spent a whole month in Kanz, which is a long time." A sign to us to leave. It was not the sheikh's habit to repeat his orders, which he always expressed obliquely. Before taking the last of a series of sips from a glass of hot tea, and while directing his gaze at a kneeling camel trying to free itself from its ties, he added: "I would not wish you to be like those poets who say things they do not do."

Abdurrahman responded instantly, whispering in my ear: "What the sheikh doesn't know, and his helper from the jinn didn't tell him, is that we are following in the footsteps of those crazy, vagabond poets."

I was unable to suppress a laugh, which aroused the sheikh's curiosity and, so it seemed, his displeasure. He asked me directly: "Did I say something funny?"

Zaydan was annoyed that someone had dared to misbehave at the assembly of the sheikh of Kanz, even if only with an out-of-place laugh, and he was visibly disgusted.

The sheikh's signal had been clear, so we had to leave right away.

We experienced conflicting emotions at leaving Kanz. I felt very sad at leaving a world where I had felt at home from the first moment. Abdurrahman, though, was happy because he had amassed a fresh stock of stories and got to know people whose lives were exotic, but especially because he had met the beloved of his teacher, who had remained in his memory a faded image since a child. Now he had corrected many misunderstandings, confirmed stories he had heard, and recorded lyrical passages of his teacher Rajab's poetry, which he added to his vast store of high and low verse.

Tomorrow, he would be able to enchant the clubs and assemblies held every evening in some of Nabaa's homes with stories about the people he had met on his recent journey to Kanz.

For sure, he would talk about Mounira, guardian of the moon and stars in the desert night. He would talk about her with no hint of the embarrassment that usually afflicts men when they talk about women to their seniors, who might hide their secrets in a bottomless well.

* * *

We headed for Nabaa in an ancient Land Rover driven by an elderly man with a reputation for navigating the Saharan wastes in a vehicle as old as he was.

The driver's name was Khalli and whenever he started the Land Rover he shouted: "Go on, little furnace!" Starting the engine was a complicated process, during which an assistant would turn a wheel somewhere in the engine's innards. After considerable effort the engine would roar into life and at that point Khalli would bang both hands on the middle of the steering wheel and shout his famous phrase: "Go on, little furnace!"

Abdurrahman wracked his brains to find someone famous who resembled Khalli and decided that he was wise like Socrates, as confirmed by his round face and large nose, which gave him the look of a Greek sculpture brought back to life.

Socrates kept us amused on the road with stories and

tales of his trips and his never-ending quest for wisdom.

We used to wait for him to arrive late at night with his passengers in the clapped-out little furnace. We would sit with him as he told us funny stories about travellers from Kanz al-Asrar, about the villages around Nabaa. And, most important of all, he brought us fresh bread and the wild mint without which tea would not be tea.

* * *

One day Khalli brought sad news. Mounira had departed our world in a mysterious way whose details had still to be revealed. It happened the year after our trip to Kanz.

"She went to bathe in the river," he said, "though it wasn't her custom to go swimming for she was even afraid of using water to wash in case she caught a cold. She would use a giant doum palm growing on the banks of a tributary of the Senegal River, not far from Kanz, as a screen, and fetch water in a large pail and wash herself among the branches of the giant tree.

"After waiting all night, they began searching for her everywhere. Not a trace to be found. All they found was the water pail, a bar of soap and a towel on top of some underwear. Strange. Did the earth swallow her up or did she ascend to heaven?"

The mystery of Mounira's disappearance was a topic of conversation for months. Abdurrahman was extremely saddened and suffered from a long period of insomnia. In reality, it wasn't so much sadness that he felt but grief that led to severe depression. The only thought that occurred to me in explanation of her sudden demise was her lack of caution when it came to wandering about alone in an area inhabited by the jinn, as had been affirmed by Zaydan and his sheikh, with whose opinion I concurred before we had gone our separate ways.

The sheikh must have known the secret behind Mounira's disappearance, but he did not disclose it.

I knew there was a lot to the sheikh and his disciple Zaydan, and I heard about an amazing incident that had happened to Zaydan only a few days before Mounira vanished. Returning from a trip, he came to the waterway separating Kanz from the dry land, which travellers crossed by means of a wooden boat. It was a Friday, evening time, and the boatsmen weren't there. As if from nowhere, a figure suddenly appeared in front of Zaydan and took him across in the boat. At the other bank, the figure refused to accept any payment.

Fantasy and fact intertwined in Zaydan's mind, but when he reached the sheikh, he wanted to tell him the story. The sheikh, however, beat him to it: "Did you find someone to bring you to us?" he said, smiling. Then Zaydan realised that it had been the sheikh's pupil, the jinni, who had undertaken that arduous task. The supernatural jinni who could do the impossible.

The search for Mounira's body continued for a week, but an oblique word from the sheikh via his disciple

Zaydan brought it to an end. Zaydan relayed the message that everyone should stop pursuing the impossible. "The jinn have taken Mounira," he said. "You will find no trace of her." That was how Zaydan explained the words of the sheikh, who had uttered a more ambiguous formulation. As usual, he deciphered the sheikh's symbolic language and gave it an appropriate interpretation. He told the search parties that their task was impossible and would be fruitless, and that they should stop looking.

The sheikh's view of the incident quickly spread. People picked it up, adding their own explanations and reasoning, such as Mounira having disobeyed the sheikh's teachings, particularly his injunction against wandering around an area where human beings and the jinn coexisted without regard to defined rules.

Nonetheless, we could not shake off the shock of the news that Socrates had brought, and Abdurrahman proposed we visit the grave of Rajab the teacher and tell him the story of Mounira's disappearance. Just as news of her living had made him happy, he would surely be generous to those who told him the news of her strange end when he was in his other world. Who knew, perhaps Mounira had joined him there, and told him the story of her disappearance in full, while we remained in ignorance.

Bread and Mint

Two successive years without rainfall had dire effects on life in the region. Khalli stopped supplying Nabaa with bread, mint and news. Connections between the villages broke down. Many sand dunes rose up, forming barriers that were nearly impassable, especially for Khalli's ancient Land Rover. Socrates found that the mechanical knowledge acquired over decades was of little use when key parts of the engine were eaten away by rust and the vehicle's wheels fell off.

He also found that life on the road – his secret anti-aging ingredient, the source of his health and the drive-shaft of his hopes in old age – had begun to betray him, and he fell victim to imaginings that ruined his peace of mind. After having spent years as Nabaa's only link with the outside world, travellers brought reports of the sad state the man was in. We were highly dependent on Khalli, who created a bridge between the villages and countryside, transporting people, bread, mint, stories and secrets, whose intricacies were known only to the One behind the veil.

Khalli and his vehicle weren't the only ones the drought struck with its deadly arrows. The villages and their inhabitants and livestock also groaned in horror at what was happening. The wells dried up and the cattle could not withstand it. Most of them died and the air was pestilential with the stench of their rotting corpses. Only camels still clung on, stubborn and patient, living off the few remaining leaves of the thorny acacia trees. The camels ate salt and drank the little water that men and women hauled up from remote wells, steeled as they were with great patience and determination.

The watercourse that shielded Kanz also began to dry up and vanish as a result of the years of drought. The sheikh's jinni disciple, about whom many tales were told and, as the sheikh's disciples earnestly asserted had been of assistance to those crossing, lost his job. That good jinni who guarded the place was no longer needed because the drought dried up the waterways and created new, easier paths for travellers. Many other professions and crafts based on and from the river also died out, and most of the inhabitants of Kanz al-Asrar lost their sources of livelihood.

One hot night, there were harbingers of rain. Lightning flashed in the sky and thunder clapped. The people of Kanz rejoiced at signs that had been absent for years, during which there had been hardly any rain.

Around midnight the sheikh, as was his habit, dozed off before readying himself for the last portion of the night when he would head to his *mihrab* to pray while waiting for the dawn prayer. This time, however, he woke in a panic, horrified by what he had seen and heard. In his dream, or rather nightmare, he had seen frightening scenes that disturbed him so much he shouted out incomprehensibly.

In the dream, he had seen little fishes eating each other and a giant benign snake devouring passers-by. Mounira appeared as a young woman stealing the hearts of men, ripping them out of bodies and eating them greedily, without concern for the blood splattering around her and covering her body.

The sheikh sent a message to the dream interpreters in the villages round about, of whom there were a large number. He sought the meaning of the dream that had terrified him and robbed him of his sleep. The message, as usual, was delivered by his disciple Zaydan.

I also volunteered to take the message to the seer of Conakry. She might have something to say about the sheikh's dream, since she could read what was concealed between the lines. I was not, however, going to tell her what the sheikh had done to me, that he had kicked me out of Kanz the last time and confided to his audience that he did not want me and Abdurrahman to live the life of wandering vagabond poets.

I expected that something momentous was going to happen. When little river fish devour each other and a benign snake bites the bodies of men, that must be a premonition of a major event.

That night I slipped away from the crowd and took the overland route to Guinea, taking a taxi as far as the border with Senegal. A British student of Pakistani heritage accompanied me. He had been teaching in one of Nabaa's schools and had read widely in Arabic literature and Islamic law. He couldn't stay any longer because of the heat, the hardships of life and the effects of the drought. Along the way, he told me in semi-delirium about sundry matters: his house, the fridge well stocked with ice-cold fizzy drinks, English bread, the gallons of milk every morning, his beautiful girlfriend whom he went out with every evening, and the many kinds of luxuries he was fond of in his country and had missed throughout his stay in Nabaa.

When we reached the northern bank of the Senegal River, which forms a natural boundary between Mauritania and Senegal, my companion and I boarded a small wooden boat to take us across to the southern bank. Shortly before we completed the crossing, the prow struck a mass of mud that had accumulated at the river's edge, and the righthand side of the boat got stuck. Even though the water was not deep, I froze in fear, standing on trembling legs in the muddy shallows, with my small case balanced on my head. For some unknown reason, my impotence reminded me of Marlow in Joseph Conrad's novel *Heart of Darkness*, which was one of Abdurrahman's favourite stories, and he frequently recounted it to me.

In a plea for help, I waved my hand at a man standing

156

a few metres away. Tall and well-built, he came over to me after stripping off all his clothes except those that decency required. He picked me up like a baby and carried me onto dry land, where my British companion was waiting for me.

I thanked the man and gave him a few francs. After a hasty goodbye to the British man, I headed swiftly for the first bus to the Guinean border.

This was not the first time I had made this journey, having gone back and forth the same way many times. In a state of confusion, I wondered whether I was taking the same route as the three men on their way to life abroad in Guinea. Did the sheikh's dream warrant all this sacrifice?

I did not find any convincing answers, and my mind seemed unwilling to share what it knew. So I surrendered to the desire to go on through the unknown African wilds. The outlines of a complex adventure were slowly becoming clearer. Had I decided on this in order to fathom a mysterious truth hinting at something momentous awaiting me at the end of the road?

At the waystation on the border between Senegal and Guinea, as I searched for the buses to Conakry, I was pulled out of my premonitions by a familiar and friendly-sounding voice calling to me. I turned around and saw a man whose features I could not immediately make out. Although he was wearing Fulani dress, his bearing and colour were not Fulani. As soon as he came towards me, I realised he was Saeed, the *sherif*'s son, whom his father had told me about and whom I had met in passing on my return journey from Labé.

We embraced each other without the need for words. Then, in a mixture of broken Arabic and even more broken French, he told me that his father had died and that he was going to inform the people of Nabaa about this.

I was unable to hold back the tears, which came in floods.

This sudden death buried my dream of returning to Labé and building another life among the Fulani women, as the *sherif* had wished for me.

I said farewell to Saeed and continued my journey to Conakry on a battered bus. In my mind, I replayed the images of my previous trip to Labé, scene by scene, as if I were trying to block out the landmarks on my present route, which was replete with surprises.

I reached Conakry at dawn the next day and stumbled my way towards the fortune teller in the poor Manéah district. I found a locked door and a deserted house.

I banged on the door and shouted at the top of my voice for a long time. As if the gates of heaven had suddenly opened, a feeble voice – an old woman's, it became clear subsequently – addressed me. She had got out of bed after my continuous knocking at the wooden door threatened to deafen her.

Looking at me from a next-door building, she repeated in gibberish mixed with Arabic words that I deciphered with great difficulty: "The woman is dead.

Dead. Dead, I tell you."

"Has anyone inherited her secret?" I asked in a mix of Arabic and the Fulani I had picked up in Guinea. The old woman turned her face away and disappeared inside without answering.

My only hope was to return to Nabaa, I told myself in consolation, as I sought to lessen the disappointment and frustration. Perhaps there I would find an explanation for the sheikh's disturbing dream.

* * *

Saeed reached Nabaa bearing the sad news. At a re-markable moment shortly before the noon prayer, he stood in the middle of the mosque, tall, copper-skinned, with the handsome features he had inherited from his mother, and said he had come to announce his father's death. He spoke in broken Arabic, then unintelligibly in the language of the Fulani.

Noticing the bafflement on faces, a Senegalese student studying the sciences of Islamic law volunteered to translate the speech. If he hadn't been there, the details of the *sherif*'s deathbed testament, which he had com-mended his son to deliver to the people of Nabaa, would have been lost.

Saeed was determined to fulfil his promise to his father and had crossed deserts and rivers from the jungles of Guinea to reach this remote part of the Mauritanian Sahara.

As rendered by the Senegalese translator, the man, who was meeting his relatives for the first time, said: "The *sherif* asked me to tell you that he wished to return, but his commitments as sheikh of a Sufi order prevented him. He also wished to return to you Ould al-Taher, a son of Nabaa, who is now old and has no home. He has been living as a wanderer between the villages and the countryside. But he did not listen to my father, who could not persuade him even to marry, a practice of the prophet that is enjoined. My father went to him, bringing a young woman to care for him and be his refuge in old age, but he received her coldly.

"As for Mohammed al-Hafez, he persuaded him to come back to you, and the man assembled his sons and daughters and told them of his final decision to return to Nabaa, to be buried in its soil.

"Such were my father's dearest desires. Some came true and others he failed to fulfil. He instructed us to make him a grave behind Hajj Karamoko, and this wish has come true, and his family accepted it with open hearts."

Saeed concluded by saying that he had passed on the testament of his father, word for word, out of filial respect for him as sheikh, including his burial beside Hajj Karamoko behind the Grand Mosque in Labé.

Saeed went outside, followed by the crowd. The spectacle of him dressed in trousers and a short-sleeved shirt and taking out a pack of American Camel cigarettes was indeed no ordinary sight. He chain-smoked in the precincts of the mosque, causing a cloud of acrid bluish smoke to envelop him. Then he passed out and was carried into the nearest house.

Saeed was laughing and raving deliriously, mixing strange accents and languages and making sexual allusions that caused the old men who had accompanied him to withdraw in embarrassment. Only the youths who had come in to watch his hysterical laughter remained.

The dream of the sheikh of Kanz began to reveal its secrets. Successive years of drought forced the sheikh and his disciples to abandon Kanz. Such is life, an eternal struggle between the burning fire of the sun and the hidden water that the clouds plant in the depths of the sand.

The Sheikh's Vision Comes True

The dream of the sheikh of Kanz began to reveal its secrets. Successive years of drought had desiccated crops, dried up udders, sucked up rivers, spread disease and pests, and caused many people to die of starvation. The cycle of military men ruling the country ground on. The sheikh considered all this to be signs of the coming Day of Judgement and imminent Resurrection.

He decided to abandon Kanz and make for Nabaa. He prayed for guidance and asked God to make things easy and grant success. He visited the cemetery and informed the dead of his decision, as he bade them farewell one by one and asked for their mercy and forgiveness.

Early in the morning, the sheikh got into the Land Rover with the rest of his family. He sat in the front next to the driver, and apart from a low murmuring of prayers and verses from the Qur'an, he was silent.

For him to leave his beloved Kanz was a true ordeal, but he submitted with faith and patience. Over the hours of the journey, he fought back tears, not allowing them to wet his beard. He did not wish to appear powerless before his women and children. How could a man who had harnessed the hidden powers to help others show his weakness before a gaggle of women and children?

Other families from Kanz had already migrated to Nabaa, choking its wide streets when they arrived. These new immigrants decided to build their houses in the open space near the mosque and along the main street that divided Nabaa in half.

The last to arrive was the sheikh himself, who agreed that his disciple Zaydan, with his bushy hair and clothes made colourless by dust, should precede him. Zaydan was singing and dancing like a man possessed and intoxicated with love. He spun around in spirals to attract people's attention to his sheikh, who had lost his charisma since leaving Kanz. Apart from his eyes, which still glowed with an otherworldly light, the sheikh seemed exhausted, as if he had lost his power to influence.

With his slightly tanned white complexion, short stature, thin body, and carefully trimmed, black-dyed beard, his strange appearance now made him look most like a Syrian cleric.

The sheikh chose a section of the main street close to the mosque on which to build his house. As if in a dream, in no more than a few days, the walls had soon risen high. Then, as was customary, the village folk came to help build the roof using corrugated metal sheets, palm fronds and mud mixed with lime. After consultations, however, they dropped the use of old-style construction materials and opted for reinforced concrete.

* * *

The day for building the roof was like a holiday, with a splendid party at which sheep were slaughtered and roasted, then offered to guests on large circular metal trays. The women prepared tea and *zreig*, a highly sweetened mix of water and buttermilk. Workers from the neighbouring villages came to help carry the sacks of cement scattered here and there, and they sang as they worked. It was a recent custom in Nabaa to use cement for the roofs of houses, most of which were sloping and made of corrugated sheets to assist the flow of the rain when it fell in the three winter months. The change called for celebration and song.

To finish, a high wall was built around the house, so narrowing the street that it was almost entirely blocked, and thereby preventing worshippers from reaching the mosque. Some dared to voice harsh criticism against a man who claimed to guide the people to the true way, while blocking the path to God's house. Others made excuses for the sheikh, whose village at the mouth of the river had been destroyed by drought and a bad dream.

Over time, the rhythm of the sheikh's life in Nabaa changed. He no longer went out and was only rarely seen behind the walls of his house. Even his temperament changed. He grew angry for the most trivial reasons and quarrelled with his wives, sometimes even hitting them, to the great outrage of Nabaa's folk, who did not practise polygamy, let alone wife-beating.

The only person who took the sheikh out of his isolation was his loyal disciple, Zaydan. It was he who brought him news and told him funny stories and jokes. He sometimes sang him stanzas that reminded him of his abandoned village. And those stanzas undoubtedly ignited the flames of nostalgia in the recesses of the sheikh's memory.

The sheikh's women felt elated when Zaydan crossed the threshold of the house. For then they knew they would be safe from the sheikh's outbursts of hysterical rage, and they relaxed a little. As a result, Hussein the poet was unable to keep his promise to the sheikhs of Nabaa. When they invited him to attend the advisory assembly in the courtyard of the only shop, he felt a mix of embarrassment and anger.

In the hours before noon, as was customary for the assembly, the sheikhs would seat themselves on mats in the shade of the walls and, to the rhythm of glasses of green tea, they would take fateful decisions. And the marriage of a bachelor poet like Hussein, who spent most of his time openly rhapsodising women, was a weighty matter.

Hussein accepted the invitation, but rather than turning up in fear and submission to the sheikhs, he addressed them with his usual boldness: "Before anything else, let me recite my latest poem. Perhaps it will reignite the spark you have lost due to the excessive sway of your wives. You do not enjoy the freedom I have, and I have not imitated that sheikh, who has gathered four young women to revive his youth."

He recited his latest poem, which expressed his love for a girl who had recently arrived with her family. They had migrated to Nabaa because their cattle had died. Nobody interrupted him as he spoke:

> Has not word of a maiden come to my kin
>> Her kiss and her embrace sweet to the teller.
> Ruddy and hardy like a camel in the heat
>> Not drinking juice, not eating meat, not married.
> Darkness having pitched its tent, I spend the night
>> Stretched out under her tent till morning.
> Free, she brings me all the pleasure I want
>> And I lack the means to marry or divorce her.

Everyone praised the poem's style and beautiful resonance. Once he had finished his recitation, which was more akin to singing, Hussein turned to the audience of his kin and addressed them, puffing at his indispensable pipe all the while: "I know that you want me to give up my way of life, get married and build a house. Just give me a little time to do all that, and you will find I have met your wishes."

The idea, he told me later, was to escape that awkward moment. His words satisfied the men, because it seemed their task was about to be accomplished. After the poet's speech, Sheikh Ahmed said: "We will lance this open boil, and the tongues wagging about a matter that does not please the tribe will fall still. That will be when an old man in his seventies stops flirting publicly with people's daughters."

Months passed, however, and Hussein the poet was still repeating his famous saying: "Marriage is a cage they want to imprison me in. And that's an impossible task." This was the last thing he said before he was seized by a state of distraction and silence for which relatives, doctors and cowrie shell readers could find no explanation.

Hussein's isolation went through stages until one day he vanished without trace. The last time someone saw him was on a grave in the migrant Bedouin district not far from Nabaa, where he would go to visit his beloved from time to time.

The slow influx of Bedouin from the surrounding areas continued because of the drought that was killing all the cattle. Even the camels, which resisted with pride, finally submitted to their inevitable fate.

The expanding belt of white tents around Nabaa caused pressure on the basic services available. Even the water pump for the well broke down. It had been a gift from the Americans after the ambassador had visited and witnessed exhausted donkeys unable to raise the bucket from the depths of the shaft to provide water for a constantly expanding village.

Abdel-Malik the butcher, tall and with an overhanging belly, lost his patience at so many requests for credit. No one had any cash and every family wanted to pay later. Abdel-Malik was used to selling sheep by the cut. He did not use scales, but cut the carcass into several parts, each of which had its known price. He stood out from other butchers because he did not write down what he was owed, but relied on his legendary memory, which retained the smallest detail of trade in a market-place full of quarrels and shouting.

The fourth year passed without any sign of thunder or lightning. Death began to prey on the elderly. Their way of life had changed, they no longer drank delicious camel's milk, and according to the doctor who the government dispatched to deal with the calamity befalling Nabaa, they had lost their main source of protein. The first to be snatched by Death was the sheikh of Kanz. They found his body lying on the hide he used to sit on. He was holding his long *sibha* with its nearly one thousand beads.

They tried to wake him up to have his breakfast, which usually consisted of corn porridge and a large glass of strong green tea, but he did not open his eyes. He had said goodbye to a world that no longer meant anything to him, once the drought had brought his life in his hidden paradise to an end.

The sight of funerals and bodies carried on shoulders became a familiar one. Tongues of sand began to extend as far as the cement houses and seemed intent on covering the village. The sands would envelop a house until only the top of the door was visible, and its inhabitants would fight every day to keep opening it. Fierce winds filled the horizon and moved sand that blocked roads. The situation grew alarming. Life was becoming cruel in an asymmetric conflict.

I felt that the beautiful world had begun to disappear, as if what fate had in store for me was different from that for all the others I knew.

Five years passed since Hussein the poet went missing. True, he had not been well, but had his outer manner expressed the truth of his condition, and was his inner world one of complete suffering?

I still remembered a line from an Andalusian poet:

To have a rational mind in this world is to be troubled
Only the mad have peace of mind.

Perhaps Hussein the poet had gone to the other world and was feeling that peace of mind which we are unable to attain. He was no doubt enjoying a new life there, whose essence we did not perceive, in another far distant place. Even my friend and companion Abdurrahman went into permanent seclusion and severed all ties with the tangible world.

I imagined him reading books, making them his only companions. That was before he departed this world, shortly before dawn as he prepared to join the worshippers at the mosque. He suffered a heart attack and surrendered his soul to its Maker, smiling as if he wished to tell us that he had no regrets about this world of ours, as was his usual manner whenever he took a firm stance at his life's many turning points.

The holy water originating from Zamzam, which had been poured into Nabaa decades before, was still working miracles. It was still active, creating *baraka*, animating hidden parts of the soul and drawing them away in ecstasy, as had been the path of my sheikh.

In Nabaa, things were happening that were impossible to explain, but that did not make me lose hope in a better future. After the seven lean cows come the seven fat cows, after the drought the rains will fall, and after difficulty comes ease.

I entered a state of Sufi seclusion and went over what I had heard from my grandfather about al-Hallaj, al-Bastami, Ibn Arabi and the Sufi ascetics, and what I had heard from Abdurrahman about Gandhi, Mao Zedong and Che Guevara when he was raising the banner of revolution in various parts of the world. Before and after that, there was the life and unique behaviour of my sheikh. He would dance when he felt spiritual ecstasy and grow angry when God's commands were violated.

I remained a prisoner of my dreams. I pondered the fates that had made the sheikh of Kanz begin a new chapter in Nabaa before he said goodbye to life.

I thought too about Mohammed al-Hafez leaving his paradise in Guinea to live in darkness and dust. I nearly cursed the *sherif* who had paved the way for him and made the idea of returning to his roots beautiful. Despite all the dust that had seeped inside me, I had not forgotten the bitterness of absence, after many sons of Nabaa had suddenly left. All of them had their reputation, and only today did they tell me that the death of al-Bahi Mohamed in Casablanca had been announced on the radio. He too had dreamed of returning in search of the warmth of reunion with loved ones. Now instead, he would meet them in the other realm.

Thus, I lived the pleasure of friendship and the sweetness of love along with the bitterness of abandonment. I had loved more than one woman, white, black, red and yellow, fat, slender, and thin as lofty palm trees. I had secluded myself in luxury hotels and goat-hair tents in desolate deserts.

Money had not been my goal. Much of it passed through my hands, but it was not of great interest. As they say in Nabaa after every prayer time: "O Lord, make not this world our greatest concern, nor the extent of our knowledge." It was as if that prayer had been targeted at me personally, so that making money had not been an obsession, even if circumstance and fate had helped me do it.

I almost fell into the final trap of love when I thought about getting involved with Hussein the poet's former lover. She became a widow before even getting married. From the outset, the affair was just a favour to that girl, who had become attached to a seventy-year-old whose only profession was artistry with words.

A secret chemistry existed between us, and suddenly that girl with a radiant face, glowing smile and slender body began to occupy my mind. She nearly came to replace my childhood friends and the companions on the road with whom I had lived the sweetness of this life, but who had left it and abandoned me without warning.

The girl kept appearing to me, whether dreaming or awake. I imagined myself innocently caressing her and her submitting to me without concern. I very nearly married her, getting hitched according to religion and law, as was the custom of the people of Nabaa, who do not like the grey area between permitted and forbidden. Fate, however, wished for the girl to fall victim to the greed of a member of the ruling military council, who had come to inspect the condition of drought victims. As soon as he laid eyes – God blind them – on her, he became crazy and decided to marry her despite the age difference between them.

I tried to warn her family and convince them that their daughter's situation in that man's house with his three other wives and one hundred mistresses would be like the state of the nation since his kind had become its rulers. The drought was more merciful than they were. I said that according to religion and law, marrying an oppressor could only be wrong, and that I would resort to the judiciary to annul the marriage if it went ahead. I actually did that, but without success! Another disappointment to be added to those darkening my record, which was already full of joys and griefs.

Here I am pitched around by ideas, gripped by obsession, living a fantasy life. I look up at the pure night sky lit by thousands of stars in a dark blue vault. One star catches my attention. It is red and blue, unusual for a star. I think perhaps life is sweet somewhere in God's vast universe.

What if we had the ability to transmigrate souls and settle in the body of other creatures, as African sorceresses and some Indian beliefs hold? By saying a few words, a person can inhabit any animal and have fun without someone spoiling things. I imagined myself a white cat prowling the alleys, eating leftovers and sharing the seclusion of newly-weds.

I forgot the colourful star until the moment that I became the only sane person in a Nabaa that had gone mad.

The sun rose from the west and chaos ensued. Women wailed and children screamed in terror. The imam fled, his trousers round his ankles from not tightening his belt. When he realised he was running half-naked, he put on a pair of women's trousers that were hanging out to dry. The pious, sober imam did not sense the seriousness of the mistake he was making when he put women's trousers on. At the same time, the masses felt the Apocalypse was upon them, and they had not had time to atone for their sins.

An hour after the momentous event, the BBC broadcast the news that an American spaceship was expected to land in the Atlantic Ocean, which we still call the Tenebrous Sea, and that the place to see it from was the Mauritanian coast.

GLOSSARY

Abu Hamid al-Ghazali (1058–1111): Prolific and influential Muslim polymath born in Iran who wrote in Arabic and Persian.

Ahmed Fouad Negm (1929–2013): Popular Egyptian poet who wrote in the colloquial language.

Al-Andalus: Islamic Spain and Portugal.

al-Ma'arri (973–1057): Freethinking rationalist Arabic poet born in Syria. He went blind as a child and spent most of his adult life in seclusion.

Amr ibn Kalthoum: Pre-Islamic poet from the sixth century. Only four poems attributed to him have survived, including his mu'allaqa in praise of wine and drinking.

ardeen: Women's harp-like musical instrument.

aurochs: Wild cattle.

al-Baradouni (1929–1999): One of Yemen's most famous modern poets.

baraka: The beneficent force from God that flows through the physical and spiritual spheres.

Barmakids: An influential Iranian family that gained prominence in Abbasid Baghdad. Renowned for their majesty, splendour and hospitality. They are mentioned in some stories of the *One Thousand and One Nights*.

al-Boraei: Fourteenth century poet from Yemen.

CFA Francs: Currency used post-1945 in French Africa, including Mauritania which adopted its own currency in 1973.

Chinguetti: Town with trading and religious significance in the Adrar region of Mauritania.

dhikr ceremony: Sufi ceremony involving prayer, poetry, song and dance in praise of God.

dura'a: Traditional male robe.

Ghaylan Dhu al-Rumma: An eighth-century poet.

hadra: Weekly Sufi ritual.

hamza: A letter of the Arabic alphabet. Used here to describe the rhyme letter of a poem.

Haroun al-Rashid (786–809): Fifth Abbasid caliph in Baghdad, during his rule Baghdad began to flourish as a world centre of knowledge, culture and trade.

hizb: One of the 120 divisions of the Qur'an.

howdah: An enclosed seat on the back of a camel.

Ibn Arabi (1165–1240): Arab Andalusian Muslim scholar, mystic, poet and philosopher, extremely influential within Islamic thought.

Ibn al-Jazari (1350–1429): Islamic scholar born in Damascus, noted for his works on the reading traditions of the Qur'an.

ibriq: Ornate metal coffee pot

Kaab ibn Zuhair: Seventh century Arabic poet who became a Muslim.

Kanz al-Asrar: Fictional place whose name means Hoard of Secrets.

Laila's Majnoun: The story of poet Qais ibn al-Mulawwah's love for Laila bint Mahdi is one of the great Arab love epics. Qais gained the epithet Majnoun (lit. crazy) so mad was his love for her.

letter magic: A form of magic using the letters of the alphabet.

litham: The face veil worn by men in Tuareg culture.

lote tree: A desert tree.

meem: A letter of the Arabic alphabet. Used here to describe the rhyme letter of a poem.

Naqshbandi dervish: A follower of the Naqshbandi Sufi order.

Qais ibn al-Mulawwah: See Laila's Majnoun above.

Qarun: Known as Korah in the Bible, in the Qur'anic account, Qarun's arrogance, based on his wealth, led him to be swallowed up by the earth. See Surat al-Qisas 76–81.

Rabi' al-Awwal: Third month of the Islamic calendar, during which the birth of Mohammed is celebrated.

sarh **tree**: A desert tree

Shahryar: The fictional king told stories by his wife Scheherazade in the *One Thousand and One Nights*.

sibha: Muslim prayer beads.

supererogatory prayers: Prayers over and above the obligatory (fard) prayers and those performed by the prophet (sunnah).

taa: Letter of the Arabic alphabet. Used here to describe the rhyme letter of a poem.

tidinet: An hourglass-shaped four-stringed lute.

taraweeh **prayers**: Voluntary prayer performed after the evening prayer during Ramadan.

Zamzam water: Water from the Well of Zamzam in Mecca. It is reputed to have magical properties and pilgrims usually return with a small amount of it.

zawiya: A Sufi meeting place for worship and teaching.

About the Author

Abdallah Uld Mohamadi Bah is a writer, novelist and journalist from Nabaghiya in southern Mauritania. His journalistic career began in the mid-1980s with *al-Sha'b* newspaper. He became the West Africa correspondent for the daily *al-Sharq al-Awsat*, and later for the MBC TV channel, and for *Aljazeera* in Africa. As well as *Birds of Nabaa* (*Tuyour Naba'a*) his works include *Timbuktu wa Akhawatuha* (*Timbuktu and her Sisters*) and *Yawmiyat Sahafi fe Ifreeqiya* (*Diary of a Journalist in Africa*). He is currently CEO of Sahara Media Group in North and West Africa.

About the Translator

Raphael Cohen is a professional translator and lexicographer based in Cairo. His translations include a number of novels by contemporary Arab authors, among them Amir Taj el-Sir, George Yarak, Ahlem Mosteghanemi, Mohamed Salmawy and Mona Prince. For Banipal Books he has translated *The Madness of Despair* by Ghalya F T Al Said and *Poems of Alexandria and New York* by Ahmed Morsi, which he also introduced.

OTHER TITLES FROM BANIPAL BOOKS

Shadow of the Sun by Taleb Alrefai
ISBN: 978-1-913043-36-0 • Paperback &
Ebook • 192pp • 2023
Translated from the Arabic by Nashwa
Nasreldin. Impoverished Egyptian teacher
Helmy is deperate to find a better life for
himself, his wife and little boy, seeing no
future at home in Cairo. He dreams of
working in oil-rich Kuwait and its boom in
construction being the answer. He manages
to borrow the huge cost of a visa and is at last on his way to
Kuwait, but has no idea of the nightmare that awaits him.

*The Stone Serpent, Barates of Palmyra's Elegy
for Regina his Beloved* by Nouri al-Jarrah.
Translated from the Arabic by Catherine
Cobham. ISBN: 978-1-913043-29-2 • 2022
• 160pp • Pbk & Ebook. Syrian poet al-
Jarrah's epic poem breathes new life into
the tale of two extraordinary lovers,
Barates, a Syrian from Palmyra, and
Regina, the Celtic slave he freed and
married, from where they have lain at rest
beside Hadrian's Wall for eighteen

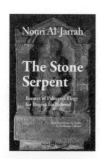

centuries, telling their unique story of migrant Syrian life, love
and freedom. Inspired by a single line in Aramaic on Regina's
tombstone in Fort Arbeia.

Things I Left Behind by Shada Mustafa.
Translated from the Arabic by Nancy
Roberts. ISBN: 978-1-913043-26-1 • 2022
• 144pp • Pbk & Ebook. This debut novel
by a young Palestinian author is an
innovative narrative interrogating the
memories of growing up, falling in love,
that force themselves to be reckoned with.
Ceaseless questioning to revisit the four

"things" she has left behind, allows the narrator to redeem her life from the inexplicable pain, loss and anguish of her childhood in an occupied and divided land and family.

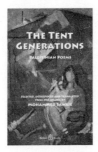

The Tent Generations, Palestinian Poems. Selected, introduced, and translated by Mohammed Sawaie. ISBN: 978-1-913043-18-6 • 2022 • 160pp • Pbk & Ebook. These Palestinian poets, most in English for the first time, bear witness to the Palestinian experience under Israeli occupation and rule of displacement, diaspora and occupation, following the *Nakba of* 1948, the wars of 1967, 1973 and beyond.

Sarajevo Firewood by Saïd Khatibi – 2021. Translated from the Arabic by Paul Starkey. 320pp. ISBN 978-1-913043-23-0 • Paperback & Ebook. The civil conflicts of both Algeria and Bosnia and Herzegovina seen through the eyes of Salim, a journalist, and Ivana, a young Bosnian woman, who fled the destruction, hatred and atrocities of their respective countries to build new lives in Slovenia. A fictional memorial to the dead and disappeared, and to the survivors. Shortlisted for the 2020 International Prize for Arabic Fiction.

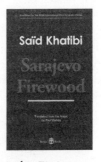

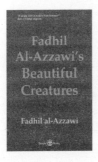

Fadhil Al-Azzawi's Beautiful Creatures – 2021. By Fadhil al-Azzawi, translated from the Arabic by the author, and edited by Hannah Somerville. ISBN 978-1-913043-10-0 • Hbk, Pbk, Ebook.This poetic open work was written in defiance of the "sanctity of genre" and to raise the question of freedom of expression in writing. First published in Arabic in 1969 to great acclaim, the author names it an epic in prose, divided as it is into cantos.

The Madness of Despair by Ghalya F T Al Said – 2021. ISBN: 978-1-913043-12-4 • Hbk, Pbk, Ebook. Translated from the Arabic by Raphael Cohen. The first of the author's six novels to be published in English translation. Living in London, far from their Arab homelands, Nafie and his wife Maliha become good friends with Dr Nadim, a fellow exile. In the twists and turns of the friendship, the men's nostalgia for their old lives is in constant conflict with Maliha's ambition to live and love freely.

Poems of Alexandria and New York – 2021 by Ahmed Morsi, translated from the Arabic by Raphael Cohen. ISBN 978-1-913043-16-2 • Paperback & Ebook. A renowned painter, art critic, journalist, translator and consummate poet, Ahmed Morsi's first volume in English translation captures the modernity at the heart of all his works, his surrealistic humour, and his visions of the dramas of ordinary life. It comprises two of his many collections, *Pictures from the New York Album* and *Elegies to the Mediterranean.*

Mansi: A Rare Man in His Own Way by Tayeb Salih. Translated and introduced by Adil Babikir. ISBN 978-0-9956369-8-9 • Paperback & Ebook • 184pp • 2020. Tayeb Salih, known the world over for his classic novel *Season of Migration to the North,* shows a new side in this affectionate memoir of his exuberant and irrepressible friend Mansi who takes centre stage among memorable 20th-century arts and political figures, but always with Salih's poet "Master" al-Mutanabbi ready with an adroit comment.

Goat Mountain by Habib Selmi
ISBN: 978-1-913043-04-9 • Paperback &
Ebook • 92pp • 2020. Translated from the
Arabic by Charis Olszok. The author's debut
novel, from 1988, now in English
translation. The journey to Goat Mountain,
a dusty, desert Tunisian village, begins in a
dilapidated old bus. "I enjoyed this book. I
liked its gloomy atmosphere, its strangeness
and sense of unfamiliarity. Eerie, funereal,
and outstanding!" – Jabra Ibrahim Jabra

The Mariner by Taleb Alrefai
ISBN: 978-1-913043-08-7 • Paperback &
Ebook • 160pp • 2020. Translated from the
Arabic by Russell Harris. A fictional re-
telling of the final treacherous journey at sea
of famous Kuwaiti dhow shipmaster Captain
Al-Najdi, with flashbacks to the awesome
pull of the sea on Al-Najdi since childhood,
his years pearl fishing and the industry's
demise, and his voyages around the Arabian
Peninsula with Australian sailor Alan Villiers.

A Boat to Lesbos, and other poems by Nouri
Al-Jarrah. Translated from the Arabic by
Camilo Gómez-Rivas and Allison Blecker
and illustrated with paintings by Reem
Yassouf. ISBN: 978-0-9956369-4-1 • 2018 •
Pbk • 120pp. The first book in English
translation for this major Syrian poet, bearing
passionate witness – through the eye of
history, of Sappho and the travels of
Odysseus – to Syrian families fleeing to
Lesbos.

An Iraqi In Paris by Samuel Shimon ISBN: 978-0-9574424-8-1 • Paperback • 282pp • 2016. Translated from the Arabic by Christina Philips and Piers Amodia with the author. Long-listed for the 2007 IMPAC Prize. Called a gem of autobiographical writing, a cinematographic odyssey, a manifesto of tolerance. "This combination of a realist style with content more akin to the adventures of Sindbad helps to make *An Iraqi in Paris* a modern Arab fable, sustaining the moral such a fable requires: follow your dreams and you will succeed" – Hanna Ziadeh, *Al-Ahram Weekly*

Heavenly Life: Selected Poems by Ramsey Nasr. ISBN: 978-0-9549666-9-0 • 2010 • Pbk • 180pp. The first English-language collection for Ramsey Nasr, Poet Laureate of the Netherlands 2009 & 2010. Translated from the Dutch by David Colmer, with an Introduction by Victor Schiferli and Foreword by Ruth Padel. The title poem was written to commemorate the 150th anniversary of Gustav Mahler's birth and is

based on his Fourth Symphony, the four sections of the poem echoing the structure, tone and length of its movements. It is named after "Das himmlische Leben", the song that forms the symphony's finale.

Knife Sharpener: Selected Poems by Sargon Boulus. ISBN: 978-0-9549666-7-6 • Paperback • 154pp • 2009. The first English-language collection for this influential and innovative Iraqi poet, who dedicated himself to reading, writing and translating into Arabic contemporary poetry. Foreword by Adonis. Translated from the Arabic by the author with an essay "Poetry and Memory". Plus tributes by fellow poets and authors following the author's passing while the book was in production and Afterword by the publisher.

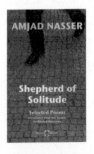

Shepherd of Solitude: Selected Poems by Amjad Nasser. ISBN: 978-0-9549666-8-3 • Paperback • 186pp • 2009. The first English-language collection for this major modern poet, who lived most of his life outside his home country of Jordan. Translated from the Arabic and introduced by the foremost translator of contemporary Arabic poetry into English, Khaled Mattawa, with the poems selected by poet and translator from the poet's Arabic volumes from the years 1979 to 2004.

Mordechai's Moustache and his Wife's Cats, and other stories by Mahmoud Shukair. ISBN: 978-0-9549666-3-8 • Paperback • 124pp • 2007. Translations from the Arabic by Issa J Boullata, Elizabeth Whitehouse, Elizabeth Winslow and Christina Phillips. This first major publication in an English translation of one of the most original of Palestinian storytellers enthralls, surprises and even shocks. "Shukair's gift for absurdist satire is never more telling than in the hilarious title story" – Judith Kazantsis

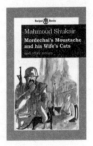

A Retired Gentleman, & other stories by Issa J Boullata. ISBN: 978-0-9549666-6-9 • Paperback • 120pp • 2007. The Jerusalem-born author, scholar, critic, and translator creates a rich medley of tales by emigrants to Canada and the US from Palestine, Lebanon, Egypt and Syria. George, Kamal, Mayy, Abdullah, Nadia, William all have to begin their lives again, learn how to deal with their memories, with their pasts . . .

The Myrtle Tree by Jad El Hage.
ISBN: 978-0-9549666-4-5 • Paperback • 288pp
• 2007
"This remarkable novel, set in a Lebanese
mountain village, conveys with razor-sharp
accuracy the sights, sounds, tastes and tragic
dilemmas of Lebanon's fratricidal civil war. A
must read" Patrick Seale

*Sardines and Oranges: Short Stories from North
Africa*, ISBN: 978-0-9549666-1-4 • Paperback •
222pp • 2005.

Introduced by Peter Clark. The 26 stories are
by 21 authors: Latifa Baqa, Ahmed Bouzfour,
Rachida el-Charni, Mohamed Choukri,
Mohammed Dib, Tarek Eltayeb, Mansoura
Ez-Eldin, Gamal el-Ghitani, Said al-Kafrawi,
Idriss el-Kouri, Ahmed el-Madini, Ali
Mosbah, Hassouna Mosbahi, Sabri Moussa,
Muhammad Mustagab, Hassan Nasr, Rabia
Raihane, Tayeb Salih, Habib Selmi, Izz al-Din Tazi and
Mohammed Zefzaf. Translations are from the Arabic except for
Mohammed Dib's story, which was from the French original.

And . . . . .

From 1998 to 2022 three issues of Banipal magazine a year were
produced each year, publishing contemporary literature from all over
the Arab world in English translation. Access to the complete digital
archive of issues is available for institutions, and a number of print back
issues are also available individually.